ACCLAIM FOR THE NOVELS OF OPAL CAREW

Reviewer Top Pick. "The emotional depth and characterization of each player is brilliantly portrayed, and the sex is enticing and steamily erotic. . . . Creative, sensual, and talented . . . I plan to get everything Ms. Carew has ever written to keep on my shelf. Bravo for a job well done!"
—*Night Owl Reviews*

4 stars! "Carew's devilish twists and turns keep the emotional pitch of the story moving from sad to suspenseful to sizzling to downright surprising in the end. . . . The plot moves swiftly and satisfyingly."
—*RT Book Reviews*

"Fresh, exciting, and extremely sexual with characters you'll fall in love with. Absolutely fantastic!"
Fresh Fiction

"The constant and imaginative sexual situations keep the reader's interest, along with likable characters with emotional depth. Be prepared for all manner of coupling, including groups, exhibitionism, voyeurism, and same-sex unions. . . . I recommend *Swing* for the adventuresome who don't mind singeing their senses."
—*Regency Reader*

"Carew pulls off another scorcher. . . . [She] knows how to write a love scene that takes her reader to dizzying heights of pleasure."
—*My Romance Story*

"So much fun to read . . . the story line is fast-paced with wonderful humor."
—*Genre Go Round Reviews*

"A great book . . . Ms. Carew has wonderful imagination."
—*Night Owl Reviews*

"Opal Carew brings erotic romance to a whole new level. . . . [She] writes a compelling romance and sets your senses on fire with her heightened love scenes!"
—*Reader to Reader*

Bliss

Opal Carew

ST. MARTIN'S GRIFFIN

NEW YORK

This is a work of fiction. All of the characters, organizations, and events portrayed in this novel are either products of the author's imagination or are used fictitiously.

ISBN 978-0-312-58014-8

First Edition: July 2010

10 9 8 7 6 5 4 3 2 1

To Matt,
whose idealism, passion,
and generous nature
make this world a better place

Acknowledgments

My usual heartfelt thanks go to my husband, Mark, and my sons, for their support and love, to Colette for her great feedback, and to my editor, Rose, and agent, Emily, for helping make my books a success.

A special thank-you to Doreen, my mother-in-law, for her enthusiasm and encouragement.

I would also like to acknowledge Pala Copeland and Al Link, who have been practicing Tantra since 1987 and work as Tantric sex teachers and relationship coaches. They offer Tantra and relationship weekend retreats for couples, which I highly recommend. My husband and I attended one of Pala and Al's retreats several years ago and I referenced the material from their workshop and several of their books in writing *Bliss*. Check their Web site, www.tantra-sex.com, for more information about their books and workshops.

Finally, I would like to acknowledge a great book I used to research flirting, *Superflirt* by Tracey Cox.

Bliss

One

Kara Spencer paid the cabdriver, grabbed her suitcase and carry-on, then raced toward the terminal doors. Wet snow clung to her hair, and her cheeks burned with the cold. The wheels of her luggage struggled over the uneven packed snow coating the concrete.

She dodged into the large revolving door, then shot out the other side toward the ticket counter. Damn, a line. Her flight was supposed to leave in—she hazarded a glance at her watch as she trotted toward the line's end—fifteen minutes. And after getting through this line, she still had to get past security, then walk all the way to the departure gate, which with her luck would be at the other end of the airport!

She stopped behind two men, each with only one small case. As she caught her breath, she glanced at the sign showing departures and arrivals. Her gaze scanned down the destinations, looking for flight 2787 to Cleveland, where she had to change planes for Indianapolis. DELAYED. The new departure time was 5:50 P.M. She sucked in a breath of relief.

The men in front of her moved forward and she shifted forward, too. If she actually managed to catch this plane, it would be the first good thing that had happened to her today. Actually, this week.

Kara had been looking forward to this conference for weeks and then on Tuesday, Jess, her editor, had suggested that she arrange an interview with some author who would be speaking at the conference. A Tantra expert. One of those guys who believed in spiritual sex. Kara rolled her eyes at the thought. As if people needed special training to enjoy sex. People had been procreating since the dawn of time. It was a physical act that came naturally and was naturally pleasurable— just as she always told readers of her sex column.

The line moved forward steadily and now it was her turn to approach the next available ticket agent.

"May I help you?"

Kara dragged her bags toward the smiling young man standing behind the counter.

"Do you think I'll make it?" she asked as she handed him her travel documents.

He glanced at her flight number and typed some things on his keyboard, then watched his monitor. He nodded.

"No problem." He attached a destination tag to her suitcase, then handed back her ticket. "After you go through security, keep going straight, then follow the signs to your gate."

She took the ticket, then grabbed her carry-on and hurried after the other travelers heading toward security.

As she stood in line, her stomach clenched as she kept

playing through the Tuesday meeting with Jess. Kara's column was all about helping women embrace their sexuality and enjoy every moment of it. Sex was good, and no self-proclaimed sexual expert who lectured people on how one must aspire to a higher level of sexual awareness was going to convince her otherwise. Yet her editor had made it a requirement of going to the conference that she interview this guy. Was she trying to nudge Kara in a different direction?

Damn it. Did Jess think Kara's column was getting stale?

J.M.'s cell phone rang. He tugged it from his pocket and flipped it open.

"Hi. I'm afraid I'm not going to make it," Grace said.

"To the conference or the flight?" J.M. asked.

"The flight. I had a patient come in late. The weather slowed everyone down today. She spent two hours on the bus getting to the office, so I didn't have the heart to turn her away."

Grace was a holistic healer, and her patients' welfare was very important to her. She often stayed late in the office, and even took calls at home from some of her longtime patients.

He glanced at the departure sign again.

"The way things are going here, you could probably still make it if you tried."

"I know the flight's been delayed—I checked already—but it would be really stressful trying to rush there, especially with the weather and the traffic. Accidents are piling up on the highway. Don't worry," she continued, "I'll definitely make the conference. I've already arranged a flight for to-morrow."

"Okay. I guess you'll just spend a cozy evening in front of the fire tonight."

"Actually, I thought I'd have a quiet dinner with Hanna and help her with the baby's quilt."

"I'm sure she'll love that."

Hanna was Grace's sister—and the woman J.M. had been intimately involved with until about two weeks ago. He'd been in an open relationship with Hanna, who main-tained a relationship with another man, Grey, the entire time. They all knew that she and Grey were the core of the relationship, with J.M. a third. While he thought the rela-tionship would be enough for him, he eventually came to realize he needed more.

Now that Hanna and Grey were adopting a baby, J.M. knew it was time to move on.

"So how are you doing?" Grace asked. "Have you been doing those affirmations and the energy work we discussed at the weekend workshop?"

J.M. had taken Grace's weekend workshop, which helped people determine the important goals in their lives and how to achieve them. She'd guided the attendees through exercises to overcome the blocks preventing them from having what they wanted. This involved prioritizing goals to determine which ones really matter, learning techniques to change old patterns of behavior, and visual-izing goals in order to turn them into reality, among other things.

"Yes, I do the affirmations every morning. I've been meditating several times a day."

His goal had been to bring the perfect woman into his life. Perfect for him. In the time he'd spent with Hanna and Grey, he'd come to realize how much he wanted to be in a loving relationship. One where he was the most important man in his lover's life. J.M. wanted someone who loved him as much as Hanna loved Grey.

He'd always had women who wanted to experience sex with a Tantra master, but he'd finally figured out that's not what he wanted. He wanted a woman who wanted him because she was attracted to J.M. the person, not because she wanted to experience a sexual expert.

A woman raced by him, the wheels of her carry-on clattering along behind her. He glanced up and . . .

Her long, glossy, dark brown hair swirled over her shoulders and cascaded down her back. Beneath her open coat he could see her tailored, trim-fitting suit, which accentuated her slim waist. She slowed, then glanced around, saw the number over the gate, and stopped. Her blue eyes flashed with life, and he could feel her lively energy crackling through him.

Sparks danced along his nerve endings and a swirl of heat spiraled through his stomach.

"Grace, you won't believe this, but I think I've just found my perfect woman."

Kara glanced around at the crowded waiting area at the gate. There were a few single seats available, but she didn't want to sit crowded between other people, especially since the flight, which had been delayed again, wouldn't take off for a while yet. She noticed two empty seats at the end of a row. At least she'd have room to put her bag on the floor beside her and the empty seat meant she wouldn't be bumping elbows with someone. She walked to the end seat and set down her things, then unzipped her bag and pulled out the blue file folder with her research notes. She put on her reading glasses.

Flirting. It was a topic she was considering for an upcoming column, so she'd been reading several books and articles on the subject.

As she flipped through the handwritten pages, she felt as though she was being watched. She glanced up . . . and locked gazes with the most attractive man she had ever laid eyes on. She straightened in her chair, pulling her shoulders back.

He had a striking face with a square jaw, a strong, straight nose, and amazing espresso-colored eyes. Dark and compelling. His dark brown hair flowed in textured waves to his collar. Boy, she wouldn't mind hooking up with a man like that.

He smiled, and she dodged her gaze to the right, pretending she'd simply been glancing around, breaking their eye contact. He returned his gaze to the book on his lap. She glanced back to her notes.

When we see someone we like, we naturally "square" our bodies. Heat suffused her cheeks as she realized that's what she'd just done. As soon as she'd seen him, she'd automatically straightened in her chair.

The notes explained that a person instinctively tries to look taller and more noticeable by pulling their shoulders back and holding their head high, often pulling in the stomach and pushing out the chest to enhance their looks.

Oh, man, she had just sent him a signal that she was interested in him. Not that he necessarily knew how to read the signal. Which was good because she didn't pick men up at airports . . . or anywhere else.

She glanced at the man again and her insides quivered. He had broad shoulders and the hint of hard, taut muscles under his shirt. Clearly, she was attracted to him, and her body had known it instantly . . . and acted on it. He glanced her way again and smiled at her. Her gaze darted back to her notes.

This would be a perfect opportunity to do a little hands-on research, so to speak. She had his attention and he showed signs of being interested. She could put a few of the flirting techniques into action. And what was the harm? They were both here because they were about to get on an airplane. He was seated at the next gate, so it's not like they were on the same flight. Soon enough, they'd board their planes and never see each other again.

Okay, so she'd give him some signals and see what happened. She glanced at him again and crossed her legs at the thigh, the most classic of a woman's flirting techniques. So clichéd it was potent, one book had said.

After a moment, his gaze slid up from his book and his brown eyes focused on her. She placed her hand on her neck and massaged, which her notes mentioned would lift her breasts and expose her underarm, which apparently had very sexy undertones . . . something about pheromones. She didn't know about that, but it made her feel very sexy.

While maintaining eye contact, he leaned back in his chair, put down his book, and watched her, a half smile curling his lips. Encouraged by his total attention, she removed her reading glasses and brushed her hand through her hair, then tossed it over her shoulder. Then she placed the arm of her glasses between her lips. His gaze danced down her body, sending hormones fluttering through her. He paused on her breasts and her nipples swelled. According to the books, he would have scanned her body the second he'd seen her, but now he was letting her see him do it.

His gaze returned to her face, settling on her lips. Slowly, it returned to her eyes and he smiled. A smile that took her breath away. Not an I've-been-watching-you smile, but an I-could-make-you-faint-with-pleasure smile. As her pulse raced and her breathing accelerated, she was quite sure he could.

He leaned forward, fixing her with a steady stare. Oh, God, was he going to come over here? Suddenly, the empty seat beside her felt like an invitation. Her heart thundered in her chest. What would she do if he stood up and walked over here?

An announcement over the loudspeaker caught her attention. They were about to start boarding her flight. Thank

God. An excuse to escape. She glanced back to him and . . . he stood up. Her heart rate accelerated. She deposited her glasses into their case and swept her notes into the folder, then put the folder and glasses into her carry-on, ready to leap to her feet and head for the gate. As she zipped the suitcase, she glanced back to him and . . . he had picked up his bag. He winked at her, then turned and walked toward the gate.

Oh, God. They were on the same flight.

J.M. smiled as he walked along the tunnel leading to the plane. The lovely dark-haired woman had definitely been flirting with him, but he could tell it hadn't been natural for her. If he hadn't already figured that out, her panicked expression when he stood up had been a dead giveaway.

His smile broadened. Since she'd begun packing up her things after the boarding announcement, he was sure she was on the same flight.

Before the flight was over, he intended to meet her.

Two

Kara waited several moments after the handsome stranger had boarded the plane before she joined the line. Her seat was near the front of the aircraft, so with any luck, he'd be far enough back that he wouldn't see her board.

The line moved quickly. She stepped onto the aircraft, nodded a greeting to the flight attendant, then proceeded through the cabin. The man in front of her was tall, which would make it less likely her stranger would spot her walking down the aisle. She glanced at the seat numbers and quickly reached hers, then stowed her case in the overhead compartment.

Smiling, she glanced at the man sitting in the seat beside hers . . . and froze.

Her handsome stranger. Her heart thumped loudly.

Her seat was beside the window and he sat in the middle seat.

He returned her smile, then stood up. She stared at him, then at her allotted seat.

Oh, God, maybe she could dodge into the seat across the aisle. But a quick glance told her all three seats were taken, as were the other seats in the immediate vicinity.

She leaned back a fraction, as much as the crowded aisle would allow, as he stepped past her to let her in.

"Don't worry. I don't bite," he murmured, a half smile curling his lips.

Tingles danced down her spine at the sight of that warm, sexy smile.

Ah, damn, she was overreacting. So she'd flirted a little. So had he. Anyway, when the plane landed, they'd go their separate ways. It wouldn't matter in the least.

She returned his smile and slid into her seat, then held her breath, expecting to be overwhelmed by his masculine aura as he sat down, but instead of sitting beside her, he sat in the aisle seat, giving her a little space to breathe.

She raised an eyebrow.

"A friend of mine had to cancel at the last minute," he said. "This was her seat. I thought you might like the extra space so you could stretch out."

"Thanks."

She fastened her seat belt and relaxed as people continued boarding the aircraft and settling into their seats. The handsome stranger didn't mention anything about their interaction in the waiting area. Well, great. If he was willing to leave it alone, so was she.

After a few minutes, she began to feel uneasy. Would it be better to strike up a conversation and forge ahead rather than leave an awkward silence between them? Or would that just give him an opening to discuss it?

He glanced up and caught her gazing at him.

He smiled and held out his hand.

"Hi. My name's J.M."

"Oh, hi. I'm Kara." She placed her hand in his. Goose bumps danced along her arm and down her back as he enveloped her hand in his bigger one. He squeezed a little, and hung on long enough that she was torn whether she wanted to pull her hand free or leave it in his warm embrace forever.

The pilot began his announcement and her handsome stranger—J.M.—released her hand. She watched the flight attendants give their safety spiel with their sample seat belt and oxygen masks. The aircraft jerked into motion and soon rolled along the taxiway to the runway. Snow swirled against the small aircraft windows. She felt her stomach flutter at the thought of flying through a blizzard.

"I guess we'll have some rough weather ahead," she said. "It's a good thing they're continuing to fly though. I'd hate it if they'd canceled the flight."

"Don't worry. They wouldn't be taking off if they didn't feel it was safe."

She glanced at him and released her lower lip, not realizing she'd been tugging at it with her teeth.

"Of course."

The engines roared. Her hands curled into fists in her lap. The plane was about to take off.

"If you take a deep breath, then release it slowly, it will

relax you," he said. "Do that several times during takeoff and it should help."

Ordinarily, Kara would deny any nervousness about flying, but the warmth in his voice made her feel comfortable enough to admit the truth.

As the aircraft began to move forward, her entire body tensed. She closed her eyes and drew in a deep breath. The aircraft picked up speed and she felt her pulse quicken, but she released the air from her lungs and drew in another deep breath.

"Think of the air filling your lungs as a beautiful white light filling you with calming energy," he murmured beside her.

She tried to relax as she drew in another breath, but her jaw remained clenched and her muscles drawn tight. They sped faster down the runway, the plane jostling up and down as the wheels bounced along the concrete.

"Let the energy fill you. Body and soul. Calming you. You know you are totally safe."

The warm sound of his voice soothed her. She willed her tightened muscles to release. She breathed out and drew in air again. Out and in again. Her body relaxed a little.

The jostling stopped as the aircraft lifted into the air. Her breath caught and her fingers tightened around the armrests.

His hand slid behind her, between the seat and her body, and flattened on her back, behind her heart. Heat emanated from his palm and fingers, seeping into her.

"Draw in another breath. Let the light fill you."

She breathed in, allowing the comforting tone of his

voice to soothe her. The heat from his hand calmed her. He continued to talk to her, encouraging her to breathe. Slowly, tension eased from her. Her muscles relaxed, her jaw unclenched. The breaths came easier now as the comforting heat from his hand filled her.

Finally, she opened her eyes. They were in the air and flying high. The worst was over.

She smiled at him. "Thank you. I usually get through it fine, but with the weather and all . . ."

He drew his hand away, along with the comforting heat, and she immediately missed it.

"You're very good at that. Do you do that kind of thing for a living?"

"You mean, help beautiful women relax through take-offs?"

She smiled at his compliment. "Are you a therapist or something?"

"I do counsel people, but not as a therapist. I . . . teach at a university and part of my course covers various techniques to relax. Students sometimes come to me to seek advice on specific problems."

"A university professor. Impressive."

He shrugged. "And what do you do?"

Oh, God, she was *not* going to tell him she wrote a sex column. That was a bad idea at the best of times—guys figured it was an open invitation to make a pass at her—and she didn't want him to think she'd been using him as a guinea pig for her flirting column. Even though she had been.

"I . . . uh . . . do research."

He raised an eyebrow. "Scientific? High-tech?"

"No. More . . . sociological." Okay, it sounded hoity-toity, but it was true in a way. Sex was a study in social customs and mores. "You know, we've got a long flight ahead and I hate talking about work."

"All right. So are you going away on business or pleasure?"

Uh-oh. She did not want to tell him she was going to a conference about sex.

"Pleasure." It was the truth. Sex was all about pleasure.

He nodded. "I'm going on business, but I won't bore you with that."

"Okay, no work, no travel plans. What about family? Do you have any brothers and sisters?"

"No, I'm an only child. My parents live in Colorado and we see each other several times a year. What about you?"

"I'm an only child, too." Kara had been five when her father had left. It was a good thing he hadn't stuck around long enough to sire any other kids. It had been tough enough on Mom with just the two of them. "My mom lives in Hawaii." She'd remarried a few years ago and moved there.

"Really? That's a long way away. You must be very lonely."

Pain lanced through her. How the hell did he do that? Here they were making perfectly good small talk and somehow he made it too . . . real.

Yes, she was lonely, but how did he know that? When

her mom had moved away—even though she'd been an adult at the time—she'd felt deserted. Again.

"What about other family? Aunts and uncles? Grandparents?" he asked, his brown eyes filled with warmth.

"They all lived in different states. Everyone but my grandma's sister—my great-aunt—she'd been a widow for as long as I remember. She and I spent a lot of time together."

"It sounds like you were very close. But now . . . ?"

She nodded, not trusting her voice as the painful memories rose.

In fact, Auntie Dee had been like a second mother to Kara. She still remembered her loving hugs, filled with lavish affection.

"Auntie Dee took sick about a year after Mom moved to Hawaii."

Kara had visited her every day at first, even moved in with her for a while, until Auntie Dee had gone into a nursing home.

"She died two years later."

Kara had watched her deteriorate over those two years. For the last six months, she couldn't even recognize Kara. The pain of losing Auntie Dee, even before she'd died, had been intensely painful. She still missed her terribly.

J.M.'s warm hand covered hers.

"You must miss her very much. I'm sure you were a special part of her life."

Her jaw clamped together and her stomach twisted. She drew in a deep breath, squashing the tears that threatened.

Finally, she glanced at him. How did this man see so

much? Her usual defenses blocked nothing from him. With just a question or two, he'd succeeded in bringing out these deep feelings in her. When other people asked her about family, she kept it light. Surface stuff. But with him . . . he got to the heart of the matter. Nothing hidden.

And because he did that, she felt herself becoming closer to him. Which was crazy, because she hardly knew him. But she realized she wanted to.

She liked his touch. Both when he'd pressed his hand to her back earlier, and now with his hand covering hers. Although he was hot and sexy, what she felt right now wasn't sexual. His touch was soothing . . . warm . . . *caring.* Although she had barely met him, she yearned to get to know him better. To feel his arms around her.

Oh, God, what was wrong with her? A case of lust gone mad, obviously. And it shouldn't be surprising. This guy was hot, but he was also friendly and warm. A killer combination, if ever there was one.

The pilot made a chatty announcement, welcoming them aboard and telling them various information about the altitude they were flying at and the service they'd be receiving, which Kara mostly ignored. A few moments later, one of the attendants pushed a trolley down the aisle with dinner trays.

Kara and J.M. discussed mundane things like the weather and how difficult it had been getting to the airport through the traffic and accidents on the slippery roads. Once dinner was done and the plates cleared away, she grabbed her purse, which she'd stowed under the seat, to get her sweater. She pulled out the book about Tantric sex so she could reach her sweater underneath.

"Are you interested in that kind of thing?" J.M. asked.

She glanced at the book, then quickly shoved it back in her bag.

"Not really. Someone suggested I read it. Personally, I think the whole thing is a bit over the top. The author talks about sex as being sacred."

"What's wrong with that?"

She barely stopped herself from rolling her eyes and saying, "Please," as she pulled on her sweater.

"Well, it seems to me he's saying it's okay to enjoy sex if you elevate it to a higher level. That if you study his techniques and believe that God is part of the experience, *then* you can enjoy it." She shrugged. "I think sex is a natural act and anyone can enjoy it, whether they study special techniques or not."

"Tantra isn't really one man's technique. There are millions of interpretations and applications."

"I know, but this guy is trying to sell books." She zipped her bag and pushed it back under the seat. "I believe he teaches courses, too. He wants people to think it's hard so they'll buy into his teaching." She pulled her sweater tighter around her. "As I said, I think anyone can enjoy sex. And without guilt. Even if they don't choose to believe it's a religious experience."

The pilot began talking over the speaker system, mentioning information about connecting flights. ". . . and I'm sorry, folks. It seems Indianapolis International Airport is closed due to weather."

Several groans sounded throughout the cabin.

"For those passengers whose destination was Indianapolis this evening," the captain continued, "we will arrange to book each of you on the first flight possible tomorrow morning. I'm sorry for the inconvenience."

Oh, damn. She'd really wanted to get settled into the conference hotel and get up early tomorrow to register. Now it would be afternoon before she got in, putting her in the thick of the registration lines. She *hated* lines!

"Well, it looks like we'll have a little more time to get to know each other." J.M.'s lips turned upward in a devastating smile.

She stared at him, her eyes wide. Oh, God, now the flirting had come back to bite her in the butt. That, paired with her comments about enjoying sex without guilt . . . Damn, did he think she was ready to jump into the sack with him?

Three

J.M. smiled. So his perfect woman didn't believe in Tantra. But she had read his book, which meant she'd at least given it a chance. He was sure with a little time and the opportunity to show her the benefits of Tantra, he could convince her of its merits.

He probably should have told her he was the author of the book before the conversation had gone too far, but he'd wanted to hear her honest opinion. He couldn't tell her now. At least, not right away. There was no point in embarrassing her.

The seat belt sign flashed on and Kara buckled her seat belt. She glanced at him nervously, then gazed out the window. He was fairly sure her jitters were less from the idea of landing than from his comment about spending more time together.

Although she had flirted shamelessly in the airport, it had been clear, especially when she'd seen him in the seat next to hers, that she'd never intended it to lead anywhere.

Given the obvious attraction between them—and the fact he *knew* she was the woman he had manifested as his perfect mate—he fully intended to convince her to spend the night with him. He might know they were meant to be together, but he still had to convince her of that.

Kara's stomach clenched as the aircraft came to a stop at the gate and people rose from their seats and filled the aisle. Once off the aircraft, she knew she could just excuse herself and slip off to the ladies' room, or whatever, and give J.M. the slip. But did she really want to do that?

She watched him as he stood up and opened the overhead compartment. He pulled out her carry-on and placed it on the seat.

My God, not only was he a gentleman, but he was also observant—remembering exactly which bag of the several up there was hers. He was a sensitive man, too. Warm and concerned for others' feelings. She could tell that by their conversation. And she liked being around him. That and he was extremely sexy. The attraction between them was blazing hot, and she hadn't been with a guy for a while.

As the line of people began to move, J.M. waited for her to move in front of him, then followed her toward the front of the aircraft.

Maybe she should look at this as a golden opportunity. She could have a one-night stand—something she'd never done before—with a sensational guy. And she didn't have to worry about the repercussions, like the awkwardness the following morning when they promised to call each other, knowing full well they never would, or the potential embarrassment of running into each other again after breaking that promise.

"Good night." The flight attendant nodded as Kara stepped past her. "I hope you enjoyed the flight," she said as J.M. passed her.

The more Kara thought about it, the more she realized she did not want to let this chance slip away.

They walked through the long tunnel leading from the plane to the gate, then stepped into the bustle of the terminal. J.M. slowed, then rested his hand on her arm and guided her out of the flow of traffic.

"Hold on a second," he said.

She nodded as she watched him pull out his cell phone and tap digits on the keypad. A moment later, he turned away while he talked to someone, then he flipped the phone closed.

"I don't really want to get caught up in that," he said, nodding his head toward the horde of people heading to the airline desk to set up their flight for tomorrow and ask about hotels, "so I just reserved a room at Angel's Inn, a small hotel just a few miles from the airport. I'll book tomorrow's flight on-line."

Kara nodded. That made more sense than standing in a long line, and she knew with so many people arriving all at once at the hotels the airline recommended, the reception desks would be mobbed. It would probably be hours before they got a room.

Oh, damn. Was this good-bye?

She remembered the warmth of J.M.'s hand on her back,

and the calm that had resonated from his touch. She had no doubt the heat of his touch could elicit far more than a calming response. An electric zing spiked through her at the thought of his arms encircling her, drawing her close to his body, of those full lips capturing hers in a smoldering kiss.

She was sure he was as interested as she was, but she hadn't given him any hints. With her luck, he'd walk out of her life any second if she didn't do something. Now.

She stepped toward him and, before she could change her mind, settled her hands on his shoulders, pushed herself onto her toes, and pressed her lips to that sensuous mouth of his. An electric tingle shimmered through her and her hormones danced in delight. Their mouths parted and she stared at him, allowing the heat she felt to shine in her eyes.

At the sight of his brown eyes, dark with desire, her breath caught. Oh, God, she wanted to feel this man's arms around her. To feel his lips plundering hers. To touch that magnificent body of his.

His arms slid around her and he pulled her against him, his mouth finding hers again. His lips moved on hers and she glided her arms around his shoulders. She'd been right about the muscles under his shirt. She felt the solid contours of his arms embracing her and her breasts pressed against a hard, sculpted chest. His tongue brushed against her lips and she parted. As he swept inside her mouth and stroked, she melted against him.

He released her lips and brushed the hair over her temple. She could feel his warm breath against her ear. "I was going to invite you to share my room. Does this mean yes?"

Butterflies danced inside her stomach. She could still back out. A kiss wasn't a commitment to all-out sex.

Ah, damn, Kara, don't second-guess everything.

Why not allow herself to experience what could only be a magnificent adventure? Sure, she'd never had a one-night stand before, but hadn't she been the one saying that people could enjoy sex without guilt? That's what she was always telling readers, anyway. Of course, her columnist persona was very different from real-life Kara. Real-life Kara had always been the shy, bookish type, which is why she'd chosen to become a writer. Of course, writers needed to pay the bills, so when she heard about the job opening for the sex columnist gig, she'd ditched her glasses, given her wardrobe a makeover, and landed herself the job. Little did her boss— or her readers—know that most of the advice she doled out was culled from relationship books rather than from personal experience.

He kissed her again, his lips moving on hers in a sinfully sexy caress.

"What do you say, Kara?"

She simply nodded, unable to find her voice.

He smiled, then wrapped his hand around her elbow and led her into the cold, snowy night. Somehow, he flagged down a cab within minutes and they were on their way to Angel's Inn.

Kara stepped into the room as J.M. held the door for her. Her eyes widened at the large, luxurious suite.

"Pretty fancy," she said.

He followed her into the room and closed the door. She kicked off her boots, then slid her coat from her shoulders. He took it and hung it in the closet.

"I thought you might prefer a little space." He hung his own coat beside hers.

She stepped farther into the large room, glancing around at the soft beige couch and chair across from a cherry cabinet that probably held a TV inside. Plants and artwork gave the sitting area a homey feel. There was a doorway straight ahead that probably led to the bedroom.

She smiled. "You mean, I can sleep on the couch if I like?"

He carried their suitcases across the room and set them by the bedroom door.

"If you don't want to share the bed, *I'll* sleep on the couch."

She quirked her head. "Really?"

He stepped toward her and anticipation fluttered through her. His brown eyes darkened as he stroked his hand over her cheek. Heat shimmered through her and her heart thundered in her chest. He cupped her face and gazed into her eyes.

"I don't want you to feel pressured into anything just because you agreed to stay the night." He stroked her cheek. "As for protection, I've been tested recently so there are no worries about that, but I can get some condoms if you'd like."

She shook her head. "I've been tested, too. And I'm on the Pill."

Her gaze dropped to his lips . . . full and sensuous. Her

whole body tingled, wanting to feel his mouth on hers. Her lips parted as she tilted her head and pressed her lips to his.

Warm. And firm.

The moment their lips met, she could sense his control—as if he had to stop himself from dragging her against him and ravaging her. His mouth moved on hers with a sweet tenderness. His tongue trailed along the seam of her lips, then pressed inside. She met him, gliding her tongue over his, then dove into the heat of his mouth. He tasted minty and male . . . and very sexy.

Their lips parted and she wrapped her arms around his neck and stroked her cheek against his raspy one.

"I want to be here. With you," she murmured against his ear.

He captured her lips again, pulling her tight to his body, crushing her breasts against his solid, muscular chest. Her nipples hardened and heat simmered through her entire body.

Oh, God, she wanted him.

A knock sounded at the door and she stiffened and took a quick step back. Who knew they were here?

"When I checked in, I asked them to have room service send up some wine," he explained. "I thought you might like that."

She smiled and nodded. He crossed the room and opened the door and the bellman entered the room and placed a tray with a bottle of wine and two long-stemmed glasses on the round cherry dining table, big enough for two, beside the sitting area.

"Open it now, sir?" he asked.

"Please."

The uniformed man pulled out a small device from his pocket, uncorked the bottle, and discreetly left them to their wine.

Kara took a sip. She didn't drink wine a lot, but she appreciated the dry yet slightly fruity flavor.

She took another sip, wondering how these things usually went. Should she just rip off her clothes and jump into his arms? Or wait for him to make the first move?

She sipped again and glanced at him. He smiled.

"You don't have to be nervous. We'll go at whatever pace suits you."

Damn, she thought she was doing a good job of playing it cool, but J.M. was clearly able to read her true emotions.

Her gaze shifted from his eyes to his full lips, then drifted downward, over his broad, muscular chest, to his narrow waist. Lower to his fitted black jeans, gliding over his crotch, which was stretching tight over a growing bulge. Her gaze shifted upward again until she met his silky-hot gaze. His lips turned up in a half smile. His gaze slipped to her lips and lingered, then glided to her breasts. Her nipples swelled as he focused on one, then the other until they ached with need. He shifted lower, perusing her body with intense male interest.

"You're a very sexy woman, Kara." His voice, as smooth as velvet, caressed her senses, sending tremors through her body.

She took another sip of wine, then placed her glass

on the table. Her fingers curled around the top button of her blouse, then she released it. She dipped her fingers under the fabric and between her breasts. His gaze glued to her hand. She released the next button, exposing a little lace from her bra. She ran her fingers along the sides of her blouse, parting the fabric a fraction more, loving the heat simmering in his eyes as he watched. She released the next three buttons, then parted the fabric to reveal her black lace bra.

She tugged the blouse from her waistband and pushed it off her shoulders, allowing both her suit jacket and blouse to fall to the floor. As she reached behind to unfasten the button of her skirt, she was well aware of how her breasts pushed forward. She slipped the skirt from her hips and dropped it to the floor, then stepped out of it and kicked it away. Now she stood in front of him in only her black bra and panties.

"My God, you are . . . incredible," he said.

She stepped toward him, her hips swaying, and she wrapped her arms around him and kissed him. Her body, including her seminaked breasts, pressed against the smooth fabric of his shirt, while the coarser wool of his casual blazer brushed her sides. The heat of his body . . . the textures of his clothing . . . the hot moistness of his mouth as her tongue swirled inside him . . . all provided a sensuous onslaught.

Anxious to feel his naked body against hers, she reached for his shirt buttons and began releasing them. She drew her mouth from his and eased back. He flicked the last few buttons loose, then shrugged free of his shirt and jacket. His massive chest, contoured with muscles, took her breath away. She ran the flat of her hand across the silky steel of his tightly defined abs, then downward. He flung open his jeans and dropped them to the floor, then kicked them aside. She stroked over the massive bulge in his briefs and he groaned.

He grasped her wrist and drew her hand to his lips, then kissed it.

She cupped his cheek and gazed at him. "Don't you want me to touch you?" she asked, her voice sultry.

"I do, I just . . ."

"Want to keep control?"

He smiled and nodded.

"So . . . what if you don't?" she asked. "What if you just let yourself lose control?"

J.M. had been finding it difficult to keep control with Kara. Seeing her sexy body, feeling her hands on him . . . her mouth . . . He had years of Tantra training . . . was used to keeping control of his arousal, controlling when he climaxed. Yet one touch of her hand and he felt ready to burst.

What would happen if he just let go of control? No matter what, he didn't want to make it obvious he used Tantric techniques. Not since he knew she'd read his book and was against the idea of Tantra. Another time, when they could discuss it. He didn't want to ruin tonight with a possible argument.

She smiled and stroked down his chest. Her delicate fingers brushed over his flesh, over his abs . . . toward his aching cock. He sucked in a shallow breath as she brushed over his cock again, then pushed aside the cotton of his briefs and freed his aching member.

She wrapped both hands around his erection and simply gazed at it. It twitched within her grasp. She pressed one hand against his chest, keeping the other firmly wrapped around his shaft, then backed him up until he felt the couch behind him. He sat down and she crouched in front of him, sliding off his briefs. Then . . . oh, her lips wrapped around him and she swallowed his cockhead into her hot, moist mouth.

"Sweetheart, that feels way too good."

She laughed, then began to suck, her tongue flicking over the tip of him. She glided halfway down his shaft, then back up. He swelled under her attention. Her hands wrapped around him and she stroked up and down as she sucked. Then she dove downward, taking his entire cock in her mouth.

"Oh, honey." His cock, so hard, throbbed with the need to release. "I might just—" He groaned in pleasure as her hands cupped his balls and she sucked deeply.

She slipped from his cock and smiled. "Then why don't you just . . ." She grinned and dove down on him again. She bobbed up and down, gently massaging his balls.

He stroked his fingers through her hair as the tension built within him. He tensed and . . .

"Sweetheart, I'm going to—"

Before he could even finish warning her, he exploded in a mind-numbing orgasm.

She squeezed him in her mouth and swallowed . . . squeezed and swallowed.

Finally, she released him and he opened his arms to her. She pushed herself up and climbed onto his lap, one knee on each side of his thighs, and kissed him. The heat of her pussy, still encased in her skimpy panties—skimpy, *damp* panties—made his wilting cock swell again.

"You are very good at that," he said.

She grinned. "Thank you."

He stroked a fingertip along the top of her black lace bra, itching to touch her swelling breasts. She released his shoulders and reached around behind her, thrusting her delicious breasts forward. The bra loosened and she dropped the straps off her shoulders, then teasingly ran her fingers over the cups, which still clung to her. Slowly, she drew the garment from her body, then tossed it aside, revealing her round, perfectly formed breasts, the pert, beaded nipples standing tall and hard. She cupped her breasts, then stroked her fingertips over the swollen nipples.

His cock lurched to attention. He reached forward and cupped one soft breast in his hand. The hard nipple pressed into his palm. She pushed herself onto her knees, positioning her breasts within easy reach of his mouth. He licked one pert nipple, then covered it with his mouth. He swirled his tongue around and around, then drew it deep. She moaned and wrapped her hands around his head and drew him closer. At the feel of her aureole under his tongue and her soft whimper as he sucked on her, his cock rose to full attention.

She reached for it and stroked, then he felt his cockhead

31

drag across her crotch. The silk of her panties blocked direct contact, but he could feel the warm dampness of her pussy. Oh, God, he wanted to push into her right now. To impale her, then hammer into her until they both exploded in the most intense orgasm either of them had ever experienced.

She fidgeted, then suddenly he felt her hot, moist flesh against him. She'd pushed the crotch of her panties aside. She positioned him and drove downward. His cock rocketed up into her hot passage and he groaned in ecstasy.

"Sweetheart, you are so hot and wet."

"And you are so . . . hard . . . so . . . *big*."

Four

Kara sucked in a deep breath, getting used to J.M.'s huge rock-hard cock stretching her. It felt so . . . enormous . . . so . . . fantastic.

He sucked on her nipple again and she moaned, lifting her body, and gliding down again, taking him deep. He wrapped his arms around her, then flipped them over so she was lying on her back and he was above her. He drew back and tugged her undies down her legs and discarded them, then he pressed his cock to her opening again. He drove forward, impaling her completely.

She wrapped her legs around him, opening to him. She drew his face to hers and kissed him passionately.

"J.M., take me. Fill me with that big cock of yours again and again."

He grinned. "My pleasure."

He drew back, then drove into her again.

"Oh, yeah," she murmured.

Again and again. Pleasure built within her, carrying her

on a wave of delight. Deeper and harder with each stroke . . .
he thrust. Again and again. She squeezed him inside, feeling his cockhead drag against her every time he pulled out.

"Yes. Make me come," she cried.

He nuzzled her neck. "I want you to come, sweetheart."
He drove deep and she could feel him twitch within her.
"Tell me when you're coming."

As he hammered into her, she felt a joyous wave of pleasure, then . . .

"Oh, God, I'm . . . coming."

Sheer ecstasy washed over her as she clung to him and
moaned. He kept driving into her, filling her with pleasure.
Time seemed to slow and every sensation heightened.

When she felt him erupt inside her, her pleasure shot
higher still . . . until she reached a state of absolute bliss. He
groaned, holding her tight against him.

As her senses settled from sublime to simply delighted,
she became conscious of his lips brushing her ear, his muscular chest pressed tight against her breasts, as well as the
rest of his hard body along the length of hers . . . his cock
still embedded inside her. She squeezed him and he twitched,
stimulating delicious tremors through her.

What the heck was this all about? Usually, when she was
done, she was done! But right now, she could use a little
more of what he'd already given her. Actually, a lot more!

She squeezed him again and arched against him, pressing
her swollen, needy breasts against his hard, broad chest. His
hand stroked down her thigh and his chest rumbled with a
deep chuckle.

"I take it you're not fully satisfied."

She nuzzled his ear. "Actually, you did a pretty good job," she teased. "So good that I think I'd like a little more."

He arched his pelvis forward, pushing his hardening cock deeper inside her. "A little?"

"Well, in your case, 'little' isn't really the right word." She nibbled his earlobe as she stroked her hands along his solid back. "Big—"

He pushed in deeper and she sucked in air.

"I mean, 'enormous' is a better word."

He kissed her, his mouth firmly covering hers, then his tongue stroking inside. His hand stroked along her side, then he wrapped his arms around and lifted her, keeping his cock buried inside her. He cupped her behind and carried her through the bedroom door, then sat down on the bed. As he lay down, she crouched above him, her knees on either side of his muscular thighs, his thick cock still impaling her. He stroked her breasts, then cupped them as she rocked her pelvis back and forth. His cock stroked her insides, sending tumultuous sensations rocketing through her.

His thumbs stroked over her hard nipples. She leaned forward, offering him one. He took it in his mouth and stroked the nub with his tongue, then he began sucking on it. He stroked the other nipple with his fingertip, eliciting a breathy moan.

She squeezed him as she drew her body up, pulling on his hard cock, then dropped back down again. Then again.

He wrapped his hands around her hips and sat up, pulling her into a sitting position, too. He guided her legs around behind him until they were wrapped around his waist. She crossed them at her ankles as he crossed his legs below her, her behind nestled nicely within his legs and his cock pushed deep inside her. He kissed her, drawing her closer still. Her torso the length of his, her breasts pressed tightly against his hard chest . . . took her breath away.

His dark chocolate eyes stared deeply into hers with a disturbing intensity.

"I . . . uh . . . this is a lot like the Tantra pose on the front of my book."

He grinned. "Yes, well . . . let's just say it inspired me."

He stroked his hands down her back and she felt an incredible heat fill her. Everywhere her body touched his, heat flowed into her, filling her with astounding need. His gaze locked with hers as he cupped her butt and drew her tight against him, pushing his cock deeper. He released his hold, then drew her in tight again. Heat flooded her, thrumming through every part of her, concentrating inside where his cock stroked in and out as he kept the motion going. Their breathing synchronized and she continued to watch his dark, simmering eyes as he filled her with building pleasure. The intensity increased and she gasped as her senses bombarded her with electric tingles. She sucked in deep breaths as their bodies pulsed together, moving and breathing as one. Euphoria washed through her, then staggering pleasure exploded within her in a mind-boggling orgasm.

Once her senses drifted back to earth, she met J.M.'s intense gaze.

What could she say? His lovemaking far surpassed anything she'd ever experienced. It had been positively . . . mind-blowing.

"I . . . uh . . . That was—"

He captured her lips, cutting off her awkward attempts to commend him on what was undoubtedly the most incredible sex she'd ever had.

He placed his hand on the small of her back, then rolled her over. He pressed his cock deep into her one more time, then as he drew back, she released her ankles, allowing him to pull out. She missed his hot hard cock immediately, as if she'd lost something of herself.

He settled beside her and pulled her into his arms, then kissed her temple.

"Do you believe in love at first sight?" he murmured in her ear.

She stiffened. "Uh . . . no, not really."

He drew her close against his hard broad chest. "Too bad."

She lay quietly in his arms, ignoring the tension coiled in her stomach and allowing her breathing to return to normal.

Love? Was he insane? What kind of guy talked about love after only one . . . ? Well, it wasn't even a date.

Tired from the long day and their intense lovemaking, she just wanted to go to sleep, but she couldn't leave things the way they were. She had to say something.

Then she noticed his deep, even breathing. He was asleep already.

She snuggled into his embrace and sighed. Well, maybe she could.

———

Kara awoke in the darkness of a strange room, with two strong arms wrapped around her and a solid chest pressed against her back. One large hand cupped her breast. At the realization, her nipple puckered.

The handsome stranger from the plane. J.M.

Soft moonlight cascaded across the bed and she glanced over her shoulder at his sleeping form.

He was such a great guy . . . and they had incredible chemistry between the sheets. She'd gone into this—first the flirting, then spending the night together—assuming nothing would come of it, but now she wondered. It wasn't every day a girl met a guy as perfect as J.M. Intelligent, sensitive, caring. And he sure knew how to love a woman.

At the thought, his softly uttered words scrambled through her brain.

Do you believe in love at first sight?

Oh, man, why in the world had he asked that? Did she want a guy who would believe he loved her after only a few brief hours together?

His hand tightened on her breast and she froze. Was that just a twitch or was he awake? His lips playing along the base of her neck, sending tingles down her spine, answered her question.

He lifted his head and nuzzled the side of her neck. She flicked her eyelids closed.

He chuckled. "I know you're awake. What's wrong, Kara? You feel tense."

What did he think was wrong?

He stroked his finger along her shoulder, sending tremors through her.

"I hope you don't regret spending the night."

She rolled around to face him.

"Of course not." She placed her hand on his cheek and gazed into his dark, moonlit eyes. "Tonight was amazing."

He kissed her, his lips caressing hers with such passion she could feel powerful emotions welling up inside her.

His tongue delved into her mouth as his hand cupped her breast and stroked delicately. His finger teased the hardening nipple until she felt breathless. He released her mouth, then latched on to her nipple and cajoled. Then he sucked until she clung to his head, holding it tight to her chest. He switched to the other nipple as one hand slid down her stomach to her molten opening. He stroked between her legs, feeling the slickness. She opened for him, allowing him to slip his fingers inside her. He stroked her and she sucked in air, arching upward to meet his hand.

He released her tight nub and grinned at her, then shifted downward. Oh, yes, he was going to . . . He licked her slit, then stroked her clitoris with his finger. She sighed, then arched as he covered her sensitive nub with his mouth. His tongue swirled over her clit, round and round, then he sucked. She moaned, running her fingers through his hair.

His fingers swirled inside her as he licked and sucked her bud. Pleasure swept through her, rising faster and faster until she gasped, then wailed in orgasm.

He prowled upward and kissed her breast, then licked her nipple. She reached for his long, hard cock and stroked it.

"Come inside," she urged, her voice husky.

He grinned and shifted into position, nudging her opening and then slipping inside. She sucked in air at the exquisite feel of his large cock filling her. She squeezed his marble-hard shaft. Just feeling him so deep sent her close to the brink.

She wrapped her arms around his shoulders and kissed him. He began to move, slowly impaling her, then drawing back, then impaling her again. He thrust deep, then held, allowing her to savor the feel of his big, hard cock inside her. He drew back and thrust again. Pleasure rippled through her as he picked up speed, driving into her again and again. She moaned at the delicious sensations sparking through her body.

"Oh, yes. I'm so close."

His hand glided between them and he flicked her clit. Pleasure turned to pure joy and she wailed in yet another intense orgasm. He groaned and filled her with liquid heat.

She clung to him as he kissed her cheek, then under her jaw. He nibbled her earlobe and finally kissed her lips.

Tightening her arms around him, she kissed him back with exuberant passion. He stroked her hair from her face and held her close.

She felt cherished . . . and loved.

Oh, God, did the man really think he loved her?

And what about her? What was she feeling for him?

Of course, it wasn't love. Love didn't exist. A relationship lasted because the two people involved worked hard to make it last. It was as simple as that.

Undoubtedly, it must be infatuation. And lust, of course. The way this man made love, how could she help it? He was sensational!

Damn it, it would be hard saying good-bye tomorrow.

Kara shifted in her seat as the engines roared and the plane accelerated along the runway. J.M. placed his hand on her back and her anxiety immediately settled to minor listless-ness. She automatically drew in deep breaths, just as he'd coached her to do yesterday during takeoff. It helped that the sky was blue and clear, with the sun shining brightly on the dazzling white snow, rather than the blustery blizzard of yesterday. But not as much as the heat radiating from his hand, which calmed her to an almost peaceful state.

Once they were in the air, the flight attendant passed by with a cart and served them coffee. Kara sipped her hot drink, knowing she had only an hour left with J.M., and then they'd go their separate ways.

Was it at all feasible that they could make a go of a rela-tionship? Last night had been absolutely sensational. She could certainly learn a lot from him and that would be good for her column, but would he like being in a relationship where everything they did in the bedroom wound up in a major magazine? On the other hand, it wasn't so much what he did, but *how* he did it. How could she convey that to her readers? Could she even figure it out?

Damn, the man made her feel way out of her depth. *She* was supposed to be the expert on sex.

"You seem deep in thought."

She glanced at J.M. and shrugged. "Just thinking about all the work I have ahead of me when we arrive." In fact, she hadn't thought about the conference once since she'd met J.M. What was stressing her right now was trying to decide whether she really wanted to say good-bye to him forever.

"Didn't you say you were traveling for pleasure?"

Damn. She'd forgotten that.

"True, but I have some work I have to finish while I'm away. I need to figure out when I'll do that. There's also the whole rush at the end of the trip, like getting my luggage and arranging transportation, checking into the hotel, et cetera."

He smiled. "Ah, the fun of modern-day travel."

He rested his hand on her arm, an affectionate rather than sexual contact, but still his touch sent heat thrumming through her. She wanted to fling herself into his arms and be swept away by his potent animal magnetism. Actually, that wasn't quite right. His powerful attraction involved something more than basic physical appeal. Something less tangible . . . and far more dangerous . . . was at work.

Dangerous because she didn't understand it. His mere touch could send her up in flames. How could she deal with that?

The flight attendant came by to gather their cups.

"At least we can collect our luggage together, then . . . maybe we can share a cab?"

"No," she said a little too sharply. She shifted in her seat and stared at the seat in front of her. "I mean, I'll be renting a car."

J.M. watched Kara, wondering why she was so tense. Although their time together last night had been spectacular, he'd sensed her withdrawal from him as the flight wore on. He wanted to ask her where she lived, to suggest they could see each other again once they both returned home, but he sensed she would not be amenable.

Damn, he didn't even know her last name.

The pilot announced that they would be landing in ten minutes. That meant J.M. had precious little time to see Kara before she would disappear from his life. Unless he did something about it. Unless he could convince her to see him again.

The plane was landing, but he'd wait until they got inside the airport to discuss this with her. They'd both have to pick up their luggage, so he still had a little time. They disembarked and followed the crowd to the luggage carousels. They moved to a position where they could see the ramp feeding the conveyor, a little away from the crowd.

"I guess this will be good-bye soon," he said to her.

She sent him a quick glance, then nodded.

"Kara, it doesn't have to be."

She glanced at him again, her lips drawn tight.

"We had a great time last night," he continued. "We seem to be pretty compatible."

She frowned and his heart sank. She drew in a deep breath, then gazed at him.

"Look, J.M. I assumed you knew this was just a one-night thing—"

He took her hand. "Kara, didn't you think last night was special?"

Her forehead furrowed. "Of course I did. I just . . . don't want to get involved right now. I'm very interested in my career at this point, and the last thing I need is to get sucked into something that makes me feel . . . completely out of control."

"So what if you do?" he asked with a smile. "What if you just let yourself lose control?"

It took Kara a moment to realize he was repeating what she'd said to him at the hotel. She smiled back but averted her gaze.

The hum of machinery signaled the imminent arrival of their baggage. A big brown suitcase appeared on the moving ramp, making its way down to the conveyor belt. A few seconds later, a navy duffel bag appeared, followed by a red suitcase.

Kara stepped toward him. "I'm sorry."

She tipped her head up and cupped his cheeks, then pressed her lips to his in a kiss. He wrapped his arms around her, savoring the feel of her body pressed the length of his. Their lips moved together in a passionate acknowledgment of their intense attraction.

How could she ignore what they had together?

She drew away, her sapphire eyes filled with sadness and, possibly, regret. She glanced at the luggage moving along the carousel behind her.

"There's my suitcase." She turned toward the thick crowd.

"Why don't you wait here and I'll grab it for you. Which one is it?"

"Thanks. It's the black one. Right beside those two burgundy ones."

He eased through the crowd toward the carousel, keeping ahead of the moving bag.

What was he going to do? How could he let her just walk out of his life?

He drew in a deep, calming breath. *If it is meant to be, it will be. Spirit will find a way to make it work.*

He stepped to the side of the carousel and reached for the bag, then dragged it to the floor. He checked that her name was on the tag, then moved back through the crowd until he'd returned to her.

"Thank you." She pulled up the handle on the suitcase and set her carry-on on top. "I better get going."

He stroked her cheek, then drew her in for another kiss. She melted against him, her lips moving on his with a hunger that matched his own. Then she eased away.

"Good-bye." She grabbed the handle of her bag, turned around, and strode away without a backward glance.

He watched his perfect woman walk calmly out of his life.

"Good-bye, Kara Spencer from White Haven."

He grinned. Luggage tags were wonderful things.

Kara tossed her bag into the cab and slumped back in the seat as the cabbie pulled onto the road. She stared out at the snowy landscape, glistening in the sunlight, and sighed.

She'd never see J.M. again. Had she made the right decision? Her fists clenched in her lap. Damn it, she couldn't go
second-guessing herself now. Sure, the sex had been great,
but she barely knew the guy. It had only been a one-night
thing. The fact that he'd managed to throw her emotions
into a state of chaos after a simple, ordinary fling just went
to show that cutting and running was the smartest way to
go. And if Kara was anything, she was a smart, indepen-
dent woman.

The cab pulled up in front of the hotel. She paid the
driver and went inside. Twenty minutes later, she clicked
open the door to her room on the seventeenth floor. After
unpacking and relaxing for a bit, she decided she should go
down and register for the conference. She grabbed her
shoulder bag and headed out the door.

A woman wearing a dove-gray skirt made of fine wool
and a matching silk blouse walked along the hall in front of
her. Her short, wavy, dark blond hair bounced softly as she
walked. They both turned the corner toward the elevator
and the other lady pushed the call button. She glanced at
Kara and smiled. The color of the blouse set off the woman's
blue-gray eyes quite nicely.

"Hi." The stranger smiled at Kara. "You here for the
conference?"

The elevator doors whooshed open and they both
stepped inside.

"That's right. I'm just going to register."

"Me, too." She stuck out her hand. "My name's Grace."

Kara shook Grace's hand. "I really wanted to register

46

yesterday, but our flight couldn't get in because of the weather. I just got in a couple of hours ago."

"I just got in today, too. With the weather so bad yesterday, I just postponed my flight."

"Good move."

The doors opened at the lobby and Kara followed Grace from the elevator. Kara glanced around for a sign listing the events going on in the hotel. Grace spotted it at the same time as Kara.

"Looks like we're up two levels," Kara said. They walked toward the escalator and traveled up, then approached a table with a big sign saying REGISTRATION FOR SSC.

SSC. Sensational Sex Conference. Kara leaned toward Grace. "I guess they didn't want a big sign stating this was a sex conference. They'd probably get all kinds of guys propositioning the women at the table."

Grace laughed. "You're probably right. You know, they're having a Sex-a-la-Gala show here at the same time, so there could be some confusion."

"I hadn't heard that. Why would they do that?"

Sex-a-la-Gala was an adult trade show that took place in several cities across different weeks over the winter.

"For the vendors. Many of the workshops at the SSC will talk about how to use sex toys to help enhance your sex life, so they thought it would be a good match. That way the attendees here will have a place they can go and see what's available firsthand. Especially being away from their home environment, where they might feel more uncomfortable shopping for intimate devices."

"You sound like a health practitioner."

Grace smiled. "That I am."

The person in front of them in line moved forward and Grace and Kara took a step up. Now they were at the front of the line.

"Hey, would you like to grab dinner after this?" Grace asked.

"That would be great." Kara smiled. She'd been dreading attending a conference alone, but she'd only just arrived and had already made a friend. Things were looking pretty good.

"A friend of mine is supposed to be joining me, but I haven't heard from him yet. That okay with you?"

"Sure. The more the merrier."

One of the women at the registration table waved them forward. She took their names, marked them off on her list, then handed them each a name tag in a clear plastic sleeve on a red lanyard and a tote bag.

"The schedule's inside there, along with a few goodies. Breakfast is at eight tomorrow morning in the Lotus Room, just around the corner and to the right." The woman pointed down the corridor.

"Thanks." Kara turned and walked beside Grace as they moved away from the line toward the escalator. She glanced down at her bag. "I'm almost afraid to see what 'goodies' she was referring to."

Grace laughed as she peered inside. "I'm sure there's nothing too . . . Oh!"

Five

"What is it?" Kara asked.

Grace stopped as she pulled out a little cellophane package and held it on her palm. Whatever was inside was silver and about two inches long.

"It's a small bullet vibrator."

Kara opened her tote bag and pulled out an identical device. She'd just been joking when she'd made that remark. "Well, I certainly won't be lonely tonight."

"Oh, I'm sure you can do better than that little thing." Grace nudged Kara's arm. "In fact, my friend Jeremy is pretty sexy and"—she grinned broadly—"he's a Tantra master. I could put in a good word for you."

Ah, damn. Tantra again. In fact, Jeremy Smith was the name of the author she was supposed to interview.

"Is his last name Smith?"

"Yes. Do you know him?"

"No," Kara said, "but I'm supposed to interview him for the magazine I work for."

"Really? Well, that's exciting. This will give you a chance to talk with him casually. That's a good thing, right?"

"Sure."

Except that the last thing Kara wanted was to spend any more time than necessary talking with a Tantra expert.

J.M. took the tote bag the woman behind the table handed him, thanked her, then turned to leave. As he walked past the line, he saw a familiar face, his old friend Quinn, who stood chatting to a young woman a few yards away.

"Quinn." J.M. walked toward him.

His tall, sandy-haired friend glanced up and smiled. He held out his hand and J.M. shook it, then Quinn pulled him into a bear hug.

"Emma, this is Jeremy Smith, an old friend of mine."

J.M. always went by his full name at conferences like this because he was usually speaking and promoting his books. His friends understood that.

"Nice to meet you," the pretty blonde said. She shook his hand. "You're doing a workshop on Tantra tomorrow."

"That's right." Was his workshop that popular?

"Emma is the conference coordinator, so a good person to get to know," Quinn said.

Trust Quinn to find the most influential person around. And attractive, too.

"I'll leave you two to catch up." Emma smiled at Quinn. "So, lunch tomorrow?"

Quinn smiled his devilish knock-the-ladies-dead smile. "I'm looking forward to it."

When she turned and walked away, Quinn made no attempt to hide his frank admiration for the gentle sway of her behind.

"So how many dates have you made already?" J.M. asked.

"Oh, just the one. But the night is still young." Quinn slapped J.M.'s back, then settled his arm over his shoulder and propelled them toward the escalators. "So . . . dinner? I heard there's a great little pub just around the corner that serves a fabulous prime rib."

"I already made plans with a friend of mine."

"Man or woman?"

J.M. smiled. "Woman, but as I said, she's a friend."

"Okay, then. Invite her along."

They stepped onto the down escalator. J.M. tugged his cell phone from his pocket and typed in a text message to Grace's number. "What's the name of the place?"

"It's called the Waterford Pub. Two blocks east."

Ran into a friend. Mind if he joins us for dinner? Heading to the Waterford Pub.

—*J.M.*

About fifteen minutes later, J.M. walked along the street, snow crunching under his boots as a blustery wind chilled his face.

"It's just another block," Quinn said.

Finally, they entered the dimly lit pub, hung up their coats on coat hooks at the end of a row of wooden booths, and sat down.

"Two of the house draft," Quinn said to the waitress when she appeared.

A few minutes later, she brought two tall mugs of cold, foamy beer and set them on the oak table. Quinn took a deep sip and smiled at J.M.

"That hit the spot."

J.M. sipped his beer. He hadn't seen Quinn in about three years when they'd attended a seminar together on Kama Sutra, but they kept in touch a little over e-mail.

"So how's it going with that interesting romantic arrangement you had going on?" Quinn asked.

J.M. didn't tell a lot of people about Hanna and Grey and him—most wouldn't understand—but Quinn was different.

"Well, it's essentially over."

Quinn's eyebrows arched upward. "She booted you out?"

"No—"

"*He* booted you out?"

J.M. chuckled. "Nothing like that. They decided to have a baby—"

"I thought the guy couldn't. That's why they'd had problems before."

"Grey can't have kids, that's true, but they decided to adopt."

"Ah, and you thought you'd be in the way."

"I think they need time to bond as a family."

"Hogwash."

J.M.'s eyebrows rose. "I beg your pardon?"

Quinn leaned across the table and locked him in a visual grip. "I said hogwash. Having you around won't affect a baby. In fact, I bet they'd love extra help around the house to take care of the little one . . . or help with meals or laundry and all that stuff." Quinn pointed a finger at J.M. "If you're not in that relationship, it's because you don't want to be."

Kara took a sip of her wine as Grace placed her order for the daily special, which was a salad with mandarin oranges followed by fillet of sole almandine. Kara ordered the goat cheese chicken wrap with a side salad.

"I'm surprised I haven't heard from Jeremy yet. Do you know what time it is?" Grace asked.

"No, I don't have a watch."

Grace pulled her cell phone out of her purse and flipped it open.

"I missed a text. Probably Jeremy." She tapped at the phone. "Darn. He's at another restaurant with a friend and asked me to join him."

"Oh, that's okay," Kara said. "We can cancel our orders and just pay for our drinks. Don't worry about me."

"Of course not. I'll just tell him we'll make it another day. He'll probably want to catch up with his friend anyway." Grace tapped at her phone. "Unfortunately, that means you won't get a chance to talk to him before your interview after all." She closed her phone and put it back in her purse. "I could arrange to get you both together for dinner tomorrow."

"That'll be too late. I interview him tomorrow after his workshop."

"Oh, that's too bad." Grace smiled. "I could ask him and his friend to join us for drinks later. I really think the two of you might hit it off. Then you won't be left in your room with just that little vibrator for company."

"Grace, that's really nice of you, but I'm not really interested in getting to know someone who teaches . . . I don't know . . . airy-fairy sexual techniques."

"Really? You shouldn't knock it unless you've tried it." She leaned in and lowered her voice. "And word on the street is that Jeremy is the best."

I'm sure J.M. could give this guy a run for his money.

As sorrow sliced through her at the thought she'd never see him again, she realized she'd done the only sensible thing by ending it quickly and cleanly.

"If you're not interested in Tantra, why are you interviewing Jeremy?" asked Grace.

"My editor set up the interview. I . . . write a column on sex for *Urban Woman* magazine." At the nagging tension about her job, her stomach coiled into a knot.

Grace sipped her wine and watched Kara.

"Obviously, you're not happy about that."

"Not really. Not just because she gave me an assignment I'm not thrilled with—that's part of the job—but because . . . I'm afraid she thinks my column is getting stale. There are a lot of people who would love to have a column in this magazine. People with amazing writing credits . . . , with great ideas."

Bliss

"But sex sells. And you're good at what you do, right?"

"Uh . . . sure. I guess."

"Well, there's your problem right there. You need to believe in yourself."

J.M. returned Quinn's stare.

"Well, it's true I didn't want to be the outsider. The third wheel."

Quinn nodded. "You want a woman of your own. I can understand that."

"And what about you?" J.M. asked. "What are you up to these days?"

"Actually, I was hoping to pick your brain for a project I'm doing."

J.M.'s brow furrowed. "And what is that?"

"I'm writing another book. *Kama Sutra for Three.*"

"You're kidding? Hasn't that been done?"

"No." He thudded his hand on the table in emphasis. "I was surprised, too. There are all kinds of Kama Sutra books out there, from versions for two men to Kama Sutra for cats, but nothing for threesomes."

"Leave it to you to find a niche market like that."

"You bet. And the research is bound to be a blast. If you can hook me up in a threesome, I'd be eternally grateful."

"There is this one woman, actually—Hanna's sister. She's here at the conference."

He definitely got the idea Grace would like to try a threesome, and he thought she and Quinn would hit it off, but they'd need to find a third. He definitely would not get

55

involved . . . not with Grace. She was almost like his own sister now.

"Great. Can you set us up?"

"I'll introduce you, but don't assume she'll want to jump into it. I just think she might be interested. And you'll need to work out the other guy."

"What? You don't want to jump into the sack with your ex-girlfriend's sister?"

"Uh . . . no."

Quinn chuckled. "Too bad. It would have made it so much easier."

Kara sat at the round table in her room and glanced through the conference schedule. After dinner with Grace, she'd excused herself to come back to the room to read the workshop descriptions and decide which to go to. The conference didn't officially start until Monday morning, so tomorrow was a special early-bird day with a choice between two half-day sessions in the morning and two in the afternoon. Grace was giving one of the morning workshops about how to get past sexual issues and relationship problems by looking at past experiences and understanding what patterns one tends to repeat, so they can be avoided. Jeremy Smith's Tantra workshop was one of the afternoon sessions.

Kara took out her pink highlighter to mark the ones that interested her for the rest of the week. She scanned the page with the Monday workshops, and stopped at one about sensual massage. She made a pink stroke over the title. Next, she found a panel where the audience could ask questions of a psychologist who specialized in sex and had written a couple of books on the topic. She made another pink stroke.

The write-up right below that described a session on orgasms—the different levels of orgasm in women, how to improve the intensity, and how to achieve them for those who had problems. She definitely wanted to go to that one. It would give her some great material for her column.

Another that caught her eye was one on women's sexual fantasies with a discussion of what was popular and why. Use of sex toys, not just for solo enjoyment, but also to increase pleasure with a partner. Unfortunately, the latter conflicted with the one on orgasm, which she didn't want to miss.

She scanned through the subsequent days on the schedule, continuing to highlight sessions she'd like to attend, until she worked out a solid schedule for the week. Then she rose and stretched her legs, changed into her pajamas, and slipped into bed. She turned on the TV and watched a little of a late-night talk show until she began to yawn. She flicked off the TV and turned off the light . . . then stared at the ceiling. She closed her eyes and rolled over but knew she wouldn't fall asleep soon. This always happened when she was in a strange bed.

Except last night. But then, she'd been with J.M. She hadn't fallen asleep right away, since J.M. had kept her a little busy, but when they'd finished their phenomenal love-making, she'd immediately fallen asleep in his arms.

She pulled the covers tighter around her. She wished his arms were around her now. The image filled her with a comforting heat, which quickly turned to tingles quivering through her as she remembered his hands caressing her breasts and his tongue teasing her nipples to hard buds. They swelled in response. Damn, this frustration would make it even harder to sleep.

Maybe she should have taken Grace up on her offer to meet her friend tonight. If Grace liked this Jeremy, maybe he wasn't all that bad, despite his elitist attitude about sex. At least he'd do his best to please her. His reputation as a Tantra expert relied on it.

On the other hand, there was an alternative.

Six

Kara flicked on the light and slipped out of bed. She found the tote bag on the dresser and sifted through it until she found the little package with the silver bullet. She ripped open the cellophane and stared at the silver device. It was small, but she bet it would do the trick.

Damn, she didn't have any batteries. She flicked the switch and it purred in her hand. Great. The organizers thought of everything. She tugged off her pajamas and tossed them on the chair, then climbed into bed again. She set the bullet beside her and lay back, then thought of J.M. She closed her eyes and pictured him in bed with her, gliding her fingers over his hard, muscular chest, down his ridged abs, then wrapping around his hard cock. Big and heavy. Thick. She ran one hand over her breast, then toyed with the puckered nipple. Her other hand explored between her legs and slipped inside. She was already wet and ready. She imagined J.M. kissing her lips, then his big masculine body prowling over her. His hot cock, so hard and thick, brushed her slit, then the cockhead pushed against her. She remembered the heat of his body against her. His mouth capturing hers . . . then moving to her breasts and sucking her nipples . . . gliding lower . . . his tongue slipping inside her, then quivering against her clit.

She grabbed the bullet and pressed it to her wet flesh, then turned it on at a low vibration. It fluttered against her clit and she sucked in a breath. Pleasure rippled through her. As she imagined J.M.'s huge, hard cock slipping inside her, she eased the bullet inside. She thought of his cock impaling her deeply and she tightened her muscles around the device. She turned up the vibration and squirmed at the intense sensations. His cock drove deep as the bullet quivered inside her. She squeezed it and rocked her pelvis.

It wasn't quite right. It wasn't big enough . . . didn't go deep enough. She drew it out and pressed it against her clit. She imagined J.M.'s arms around her, his hard body against hers as his cock drove deep. The little device continued to quiver against her clit. Intense, sharp pleasure spiked through her and she sucked in air. She thought about how J.M. had thrust into her . . . again and again. How pleasure had rocketed through her, building to an incandescent flash of joy.

She turned the device even higher and an orgasm was wrenched from her. She gasped, then moaned. The device whirred.

Finally, she collapsed on the bed, spent.

She'd achieved orgasm, but it was empty at best.

Damn, but she missed J.M.

Kara walked through the atrium toward the Iris Ballroom, where Grace's workshop would be. She peered in the room and saw Grace standing at a table at the front of the room facing about twenty rows of chairs. About a third were already full.

Grace noticed Kara and waved. Kara stepped toward her.

"So it looks like you'll have a good crowd."

Grace glanced around. "I think you're right."

"Are you nervous?"

"A little. Listen, may I ask you a favor?"

"Uh . . . sure."

"I'm going to need someone to come up for a demonstration partway through and . . . I could ask for a volunteer, but I was wondering if you'd do it instead."

"You don't want to take someone from the audience?"

"Well, I never know if I'm actually going to get anyone to volunteer, and I usually have to cajole people and then they're nervous and I have to take time to calm them down and . . . no matter what, if you sit in the front row, you can be up here fast and we can keep things moving along. And after people see what's involved, others will be willing to volunteer later in the session."

"Okay, sure."

Grace smiled. "Great. Thanks."

Kara glanced around at the room, now nearly full, and her stomach quivered. The thought of going up in front of all these people made her nervous.

"Um . . . what will I have to do during this demonstration?"

"Oh, I'm just going to ask you a few questions about your romantic relationships."

"But—"

Grace smiled. "Don't worry. You'll do great. Right now maybe you should grab a seat before there are none left up front."

Kara nodded. She really didn't want to do this, but she couldn't back out now. That wouldn't be fair to Grace. She settled into one of the few chairs left in the front row, off to the right.

The session started and Grace introduced herself and the fact she was a natural healer. She mentioned several techniques she used that Kara had never heard of, like craniosacral something-or-other and NET, or Neuro Emotional Technique, which helped release emotional stress stuck in the body that stopped people from achieving goals. Kara wasn't interested in all the details of what a naturopath did, or the energy mumbo jumbo. She doodled in her notebook while barely listening, mainly because her stomach continued to flutter in anticipation of what Grace would ask when Kara was in front of all these people.

"So how many of you have had trouble finding a satisfying relationship?" Grace asked.

Kara immediately straightened in her chair. About two-thirds of the people in the room put up their hands.

"If you want to have a sound relationship, you want to go into it with a sound goal. So often we repeat the mistakes of the past and continue to seek the same type of partner we've had before, even though that relationship didn't work out. Of course, finding a good alternative health-care provider who can help you remove whatever blocks you have against finding a happy and lasting relationship will help immensely, but there are some questions you can ask yourself."

She glanced at Kara and smiled. "Kara, would you come up, please?"

Kara stood up and placed her notebook on her chair. She smoothed her skirt as she approached Grace. Grace pulled a chair back from the table and set it in an open area at the front of the room and gestured for Kara to sit.

"I'd like you to think back on all the romantic relationships you've had, then I'd like you to think about the list of qualities you'd look for in the ideal man."

She paused for a few moments while Kara thought about the men she'd dated and the qualities that had drawn her to them.

"What qualities would your ideal man have?" Grace asked

"Okay, well . . . I want a man with intelligence . . . a sense of humor . . . and similar interests to mine."

"Did most of the men in your past possess those qualities?"

"Yes, mostly."

"Okay, good. Now think back on the relationship you most wish had lasted. Why do you think that one didn't last?"

She thought back to the man she'd dated about three years ago. Perry. He'd been smart, fun to be with, and he'd made her feel special—at least for the first few months they'd dated.

"I don't know. . . . Interest just seemed to fizzle. We didn't seem to spend much time together anymore. He was an architect and worked long hours. And, of course, he was a guy, so he wasn't interested in any kind of commitment."

"Anything else?"

"He . . . could have been more affectionate. You know how some men tend to be distant."

"So looking back at your list of qualities for your ideal man, do you have on there: puts his work ahead of you, is unwilling to show affection, and doesn't want to be part of a committed relationship?"

"No."

"Of course not. But it is what you've learned to expect. Your choice of words gives us a hint. You said since he was a guy, he wasn't interested in commitment, and that men tend to be distant. Your beliefs about what you would find in a relationship came true."

Grace rested her hand on Kara's back and turned to the audience. Kara could feel heat emanating from her palm similar to what she'd felt from J.M. on the plane. Kara felt the tension fade from her body.

"One of the best things you can do to help attract the right kind of person into a relationship is to look at your beliefs and expectations about what that relationship will be. Find the negative attitudes you have and cleanse them with positive self-talk. Kara has identified three negatives that she would be destined to repeat in her relationships. Now she can do something about them with affirmations, meditation, or any number of other techniques. An energy healer could also help her release those blocks."

With Grace's warm hand on her back, Kara felt very relaxed, despite sitting in front of this huge crowd of people.

"So a simple thing you can do to achieve a great relationship is to picture the perfect mate, remembering to think about how that mate will react to you. You want someone who will love you, treat you well, want to be with you. Remember those things when you do your visualizations."

Grace removed her hand from Kara's back. Kara moved back to her seat, feeling extremely relaxed. Grace faced the audience and continued her talk. At the end, she took questions. After she tied up the session, people crowded around Grace. Kara stood up and grabbed her notebook from her chair, then slid it into her bag.

Grace's workshop had been interesting. Was Kara really destined to repeat the same type of failing relationship if she didn't purge herself of her negative expectations? She hadn't even realized she'd had negative expectations about her relationships. Or, at least, she'd thought they'd just been natural skepticism. Of course, Grace would probably ask what the difference was.

Could finding the perfect man really be that simple?

Kara remembered J.M. He had the qualities she looked for in a man . . . and she had a feeling he wasn't afraid of commitment. But Kara had made a break for it as fast as she could. It wasn't J.M. she was running away from, it was the intense feelings he inspired in her—feelings that made her feel completely out of control. None of her past relationships had ever stirred the potent emotional response in her that J.M. had. When those relationships had ended, it hadn't been a big deal. The powerful feelings she had for J.M., however, threatened her emotional well-being and shook her to her core.

The crowd around Grace had dissipated. Kara stood up and joined her.

"That was great, Grace."

Grace smiled. "Thanks." She collected her things and slipped them into her conference bag. "Do you want to grab some lunch?"

Kara took another bite of her western sandwich.

Grace glanced at her over her salad. "Thanks for helping me out during my talk."

"No problem."

"Listen, I hope you don't mind me saying so, but . . . there's more to your issue of finding a great relationship than what we discussed in the session today."

"Sure," Kara said, but she was uncertain what Grace meant exactly. Of course, Kara didn't think uttering a few affirmations in her head would bring her the perfect man.

"Don't get me wrong. Doing those affirmations will go a long way, but there's something much deeper you need to work on. Do you mind me making an observation?"

Kara finished her last bite of sandwich and pushed her plate aside.

"I guess not."

Kara's hand rested on the table and Grace rested her hand on it. The gentle warmth soothed Kara. She gazed into Grace's intense blue-gray eyes.

"You have a deep block about love. Something that happened . . . when you were young. About seven, I think."

Kara drew her hand away, her stomach clenching at the memories of her mother's tears after her father had left them.

"Six," Kara said.

"Do you mind talking about it?"

Kara shrugged. "My parents got divorced. Happens to lots of people."

"But it doesn't affect all people the same way. There was something about it . . . something that hurt you on a very deep level."

"He walked away from my mother. Left her alone with a young child."

"Kara . . . he also left *you*."

Kara felt powerful emotions swirling up from deep inside, but she stomped them down. That was long ago . . . far in the past. She was over it now.

"Sure. I know that. And it made me cautious. I understand that."

Grace nodded, but Kara could tell there was more she wanted to say.

Kara glanced at her watch. "You know what. I think I'd like some dessert. How about you?"

67

Kara walked into the Tulip Ballroom and glanced around. About half the seats had been taken, but since people never crowded together by choice, there were empty seats in all the rows. She wanted to be near the front so she could see this Jeremy guy, watch his body language, and ensure she could hear everything. She nabbed a seat in the second row to the right of center.

People continued pouring into the room. The place was filling up fast. This Tantra seemed pretty popular.

Sure, if you tell people there's a way to make sex better, you'll pique their interest. Tell them you can also make it acceptable and they'll flock to your door.

She settled into her seat and pulled her notebook and pen from the tote bag. She tapped her pen on her notebook, wondering what this Jeremy would look like. A woman sat down beside her. Only a few scattered seats were left vacant, including the one to her right. She glanced toward the door and . . . She sucked in a breath when she saw J.M. step into the room.

Oh, my God, what's he doing here?

She snatched the schedule from inside her notebook and held it in front of her face as if reviewing her workshop choices. She peered over the paper, worried that he'd be heading for the empty chair beside her.

Why the hell am I hiding? I have every right to be here.

She lowered the schedule, ready to face him, but he wasn't heading this way at all. He moved to the front of the room.

"Good afternoon, everyone. My name is Jeremy Smith and this session is about Tantra and how it can improve your sex life."

Good God, he's the speaker?

Anger simmered through her as she crossed her arms and glared at him. This man had not only hidden the fact he was coming to this conference, but when he'd seen his book in her bag, he hadn't admitted he was the author! What kind of game was he playing?

Seven

"Good afternoon. My name is Jeremy Smith and this talk is about Tantra and how it can improve your sex life. Most people are aware of the Kama Sutra. Many of you probably have a copy on your bedside table at home."

He smiled and a few people laughed.

"It's a popular book to seek out when we want to improve our sex life because it offers many interesting sexual positions we might not have tried before. But sex is not just physical. Of course, we think about love as greatly enhancing any sexual relationship, but what I'm talking about is energy. The Chinese call this energy Chi. The Japanese call it Ki."

As J.M. talked, he felt as if someone was staring at him. Of course, the room was packed full of people who were all watching him right now, but what he sensed was different. He glanced around the room, surveying the faces in the crowd, then his gaze caught on two piercing blue eyes.

Kara sat in the second row a mere ten yards away. Delight wafted through him at the sight of her, despite her glower. Her showing up here seemed a sure sign they were destined to be together. She narrowed her eyes as their gazes caught, and he could sense sparks of anger flaring from her. He simply smiled and continued his talk.

The two and a half hours seemed to take forever to pass, despite the enthusiasm of his audience and the many questions they asked.

Finally, the workshop came to an end and after a round of applause, people packed up their things and began flowing from the room. He had to fight a powerful urge to rush through the crowd and head off Kara before she left. Though with the crowd of people gathering around him, he couldn't see if she was still at her seat. Given the anger flashing in her eyes, he was sure she'd leave as soon as possible.

He always made himself available for questions after his talk. It wouldn't be fair to run out on the people wanting to speak with him. Anyway, now that he knew Kara was at the conference, he could find her.

Eventually, the crowd of people dissipated and he glanced up to see Kara still sitting in the second-row seat, her arms crossed. He grinned at her, then excused himself from the last couple of people, whose questions had turned to chatting. She watched him approach, her expression dark.

Kara wasn't exactly sure why she was so irritated with him. Because he'd suddenly shown up at her conference? Because he not only believed in Tantra, but was a *Tantra expert*? Or because a part of her was so damned glad he was here? Whatever the reason, annoyance seethed through her.

"Kara, it's great to see you," he said. "I'm meeting with a reporter for an interview in a couple of minutes, but will you meet me afterward for dinner?"

"Actually, *I'm* the reporter."

His face lit up. "Really? That's great. But . . . I thought you didn't like Tantra." His mouth curled up in a teasing smile.

"True. Tantra is a tight-assed prude's way of allowing himself to enjoy sex by calling it sacred. Obviously that means the rest of us are just animals who don't know any better."

A couple of people at the side of the room glanced around at Kara's sharp tone and she felt her cheeks flush. She clamped her mouth shut.

J.M.'s smile broadened. How did he have the nerve to look so damned sexy when she was so damned mad at him?

"I see. Well, it looks like we'll have an interesting interview," he said. "Where do you want to do it?"

"I had planned on the Rose Garden Restaurant off the lobby, but . . ." If they did it there, she was likely to spout off and embarrass herself and him. Though her anger didn't seem to faze him in the least, which only sparked it more. "Maybe we should go somewhere more private."

"That's a great idea." His brown eyes twinkled. "We could go to my room."

She gritted her teeth. "Fine." She didn't care which of their rooms they went to. She just wanted to get this over with.

She felt way too conscious of him walking alongside her. When the elevator doors opened, several people filed in with them, forcing her to stand closer to J.M. than she would have liked. Irritation skittered through her—right along with a tingling sense of excitement.

"This is my floor," he said as the doors opened at ten.

She stepped off the elevator and followed him to his room, which turned out to be a lovely suite. She walked past the comfy-looking couch and armchair and sat in one of the two chairs at the round table by the window. He crossed to the bar fridge and opened the door.

"Would you like some juice? I have orange, apple, and cranberry."

"Cranberry, please."

He grabbed two individual serving-size bottles and two glasses from the dresser and placed them on the table.

"So you're a reporter." He sat down in the chair opposite her, then opened the cranberry juice and poured it into one of the glasses and set it in front of her.

"I have a column with *Urban Woman* magazine."

"That's why you had my book in your bag." He poured himself an apple juice, then took a sip.

"That's right." She glared at him. "Why did you lie about that?"

"I didn't lie."

"You didn't tell me you were the author."

He shrugged. "You made it clear you didn't like Tantra. I saw no reason to embarrass you."

Kara felt some of her indignation dissipate. It would have

been terribly embarrassing to find out he was the author after what she'd said about the book—and trust J.M. to want to spare her feelings. In the end, however, hiding it had caused her more embarrassment, as she remembered how she'd accused him of just wanting to sell books. That wasn't J.M. She might not believe in Tantra, but it seemed clear he did, and with his integrity he wasn't just selling books, he was sharing an idea he believed in deeply.

"You didn't tell me you were going to this conference," she accused.

"You didn't tell me, either."

She crossed her arms. "Well, of course not. If a woman tells a man she's going to a conference on sex, he's going to hit on her."

He grinned. "So, you thought if you didn't tell me, we wouldn't wind up in bed together? That plan didn't work too well."

At his teasing tone, her hands clenched into fists and she sent him an icy glare. Which didn't seem to bother him in the least.

"Well, similarly," he continued, "my feeling is that if a man tells a woman he's going to a conference on sex, she'll think he's a sex maniac or a weirdo."

She pursed her lips together. Damn, she hadn't thought of that. Why did he have to make so much sense?

He leaned toward her. "I think you didn't tell me because you wanted me to believe you weren't in the city so I wouldn't suggest we get together."

Her cheeks flushed. Damn it.

"Look, Kara, I know you didn't expect to see me here . . . and I'm sure you didn't plan on spending the night with me." He smiled, warmth emanating from his chocolate brown eyes. "But we did and it was fabulous. Can't we just be happy to see each other again?"

She stared at him uncertainly, unfolding her arms and resting her hands on her thighs under the table. As much as she didn't want to admit it, she *was* happy to see him again.

"I assume you have to do this interview for your job. Why not give me a chance to tell you about Tantra? I promise not to try to subvert you."

The last of her anger dissipated. He was right. She had a job to do and right now that meant interviewing J.M.

"Of course." She reached into her bag and pulled out her notebook and pen, then opened the notebook and glanced at him. "I have a number of questions prepared, so—"

He stood up and gently tugged the notebook and pen from her hand, then drew her to her feet. His touch sent her senses reeling.

"I think you'll benefit more from a . . . hands-on approach."

"But I—"

He grinned. "Don't worry, I just want to show you a couple of things, then you can write down your impressions." He drew her to the couch and urged her to sit. "I'll be happy to answer your questions afterward."

"I don't know. . . ."

He sat beside her and placed his hand on her back. Instantly, heat emanated from him to her.

"Remember when I did this on the plane to help you deal with takeoff?"

She nodded. How could she forget?

"The heat you're feeling is healing energy."

"So Tantra is about healing? How does that fit with sex?"

"It's actually a universal energy flowing through my body and into yours. As a person works with energy over time, they can learn to direct it. It can be used for healing." He smiled. "Or to help two people join in a much more intimate way."

She shifted on the couch and he drew his hand from her back.

"When two people make love, they enjoy a physical bond."

She gazed into his eyes, her insides trembling as she remembered the sensational physical bond they'd shared the other night.

"With Tantra, lovers can enhance their lovemaking with an energy bond that joins them more intimately than straight physical sex ever can."

"That sounds like what people say love does for a sexual relationship."

"Of course, love is the highest form of energy, but even people in love can improve their lovemaking with Tantra. When two people are aware of the energy flowing through their bodies, they can direct it in a way to enhance pleasure. Then sex can be more spectacular than they could imagine."

"You . . . uh . . ." She stood up and paced across the room. His potent male presence so close to her threatened her composure. ". . . mention in your book about a man holding off on climaxing. Why is that?"

"To build up the energy. A woman builds energy by having an orgasm, but a man expels the energy every time he ejaculates. That's different from having an orgasm, by the way. A man can have an orgasm without ejaculation. Most men don't know how, but Tantra training teaches that."

"But I thought that . . . ejaculation . . . was the definition of an orgasm for a man."

"Most people think that a man's orgasm and releasing of the sperm are the same thing, but it's not true. With training, a man can learn to come to orgasm while still keeping ejaculation *firmly* contained." He grinned. "Which, of course, has a lot of benefits for the woman."

"When we . . ." Her cheeks flushed. "The other night, you . . . I was sure you actually . . ."

"Yes, I did. We'd already established you were anti-Tantra. I certainly didn't want to bring it up then and, if I didn't climax, I thought you'd be disappointed. You might think I wasn't turned on enough by you." He stood up and approached her, then stroked her cheek. "I don't want you to have any doubt about how much you turn me on."

The heat of his touch shimmered through her. She wanted to stroke his raspy cheek and kiss those full, sexy lips of his.

She stepped toward the table. "That's very interesting about holding off. How long can you do it?"

"Hold an erection? Indefinitely."

"Really?" She licked her dry lips. "You mean like . . . half an hour?"

"I mean *hours*." His deep velvet voice stroked her senses. "I can hold off on ejaculation for months. Building the energy until I decide to let it go."

Hours. She imagined his large, erect cock thick and hard inside her . . . thrusting deep . . . over and over again . . . giving her orgasm after orgasm.

She rested her hand on the back of the chair, suddenly weak-kneed. She didn't know whether to tear off her clothes and drag him into her arms or to fight this incredible heat simmering between them with everything she had.

When he'd made love to her that night, it had been spectacular . . . and he hadn't used his Tantra techniques. Just how good could it get?

"You told me you wanted to"—she licked her lips—"show me something."

A devilish smile played across his lips and he stepped toward her. She felt the hairs along the back of her neck prickle to attention.

He rested his hands on her shoulders. His touch sent tingles dancing through her. Her lips felt full and ripe, ready for his kiss . . . but instead, he shifted her to the chair and pressed down on her shoulder.

"Sit."

She sank into the chair and he crouched in front of her. He slid his hand down her arm, leaving a trail of goose bumps, then across her stomach . . . and down.

He flattened his palm below her navel.

"This is your sacral chakra." He smiled.

She nodded, then quivered as his hand glided along her thigh to the hem of her dress. He drew it upward a little, then pressed her thighs slightly apart. She drew in a deep breath, anticipating his touch, but instead he rested one hand between her thighs, his palm facing her body. Right between her legs.

An incredible heat pulsed through her.

"This is your base chakra. There are actually seven main chakras—or energy centers—in your body. Each affects different aspects of your being. Using these chakras, you can actually have what is called an energy orgasm without any touch at all."

Heat emanated from his hand and washed through her, heating her insides with sultry ripples of awareness. She drew in a slow, calming breath.

"If done with energy flowing through all the chakras, you can have a whole-body orgasm," he continued.

"Is that what you want to show me?"

He chuckled. "To do it on your own would require a lot of practice, but I could walk you through it. Do you want me to?"

With the heat continuing through her body, making her intensely aware of his masculine presence in front of her . . . of his hand only inches from her most intimate part . . . *oh, yes, she did!* Her internal muscles twitched.

But the thought absolutely terrified her.

An energy orgasm. That would totally negate her claim

that sex was just a physical thing. No spirituality involved. No sexual energy. No sacred-sex mumbo jumbo.

"Uh . . . no, that's okay. What were you going to show me then?"

"I wanted to show you how to use these chakras to increase your arousal. I know you don't believe in the energy side of sex, but I was hoping you would just give it a try."

She nodded. She had to write this article, so she needed to find out as much as she could. And she didn't want him to take his hand away just yet.

"Okay, do you feel the heat from my hand?"

She nodded.

"That is energy flowing from me to you. You are absorbing it through your base chakra. Now, think of that energy flowing upward to your sacral chakra."

She almost jumped as he rested his other hand on her belly again, just below her navel, heating her even more.

"Just think of the energy moving up from your base chakra to your sacral chakra." He pressed his hand down slightly on her belly. "Right here . . . then back down, forming a circle of flowing energy. New energy is flowing in all the time, joining the flow. A fire is building inside you . . . in your sexual center."

An incredible heat built within her. And along with it, an incredible yearning.

"Do you feel it?" he asked.

"Oh, yes." Damn, her voice sounded so deep and needy.

"To have an energy orgasm, we would continue up the

chakras, drawing this energy through the entire body one chakra at a time."

She nodded, enjoying the heart-thumping intensity of the energy flowing through her body. Not energy, really. She knew it was just a state of mind suggested by his words and the positioning of his hands, but the result was . . . spectacular. Her hormones were thrumming and she was incredibly turned on. She could feel liquid heat pooling between her legs.

J.M. drew his hands away and she had to stifle a moan of frustration. She shifted in her chair and felt a little dizzy. He wrapped his hands around her arms to steady her.

"So that's what you do in Tantric sex?" she asked.

"That's barely scratching the surface. I didn't walk you through the breathing. . . ."

His words faded from her attention as the intensity of her desire for him overwhelmed her. She leaned toward him and stopped his flow of words with a kiss. Her arms coiled around his neck and she pulled him against her, her lips moving on his with ardent need.

"Tantra lesson later. Right now . . . what I really want . . ."

Eight

As J.M. stared at her wide, smoldering blue eyes, so full of need, his own sexual energy swelled.

He captured her lips and teased them with his tongue, then plunged inside. Her tongue danced with his as she fumbled with his shirt. As her fingers released his buttons, he rested his hand on her lower back, then glided upward slowly, drawing the sexual energy up through her body. She shoved his shirt from his shoulders and he untangled himself from it, then tossed it aside. They both stood up and pulled her dress over her head and dropped it to the floor. His gaze slid to her sexy red and black lace bra, lingering on her breasts swelling from the top, then he glanced down her slender torso to the tiny matching panties. His cock swelled.

She tugged down his zipper and her delicate hand stroked over his bulge. Wrapping her fingers around his shaft, she drew his cock out and began stroking it. He released the button and let the pants fall to the floor, then he shed his briefs.

She grasped him again and crouched down, then licked the tip of him. Her mouth surrounded his cockhead, enveloping him in warmth. She swirled her tongue around him, triggering hot, wild sensations within him. Her fingers stroked underneath, and she cradled his balls in her warm hand, gently massaging them.

His cell phone rang.

She slipped free. "Do you want to get that?"

The phone rang again.

He chuckled. "Not on your life."

She dove downward, swallowing him whole, then rocked back and sucked. He barely heard the next couple of rings before it stopped. She bobbed and stroked, making his cock rock hard and quivering to release. But he held it inside, enjoying the sensual pleasure and letting the energy build.

She wrapped her hands around his shaft and squeezed his cockhead in her mouth. Her tongue swirled over the end in spiral caresses, then she sucked. The pleasure grew and grew. He concentrated on allowing the energy to build.

Finally, she released him and gazed at him with amazement in her eyes.

"You really aren't going to come, are you?"

He chuckled. He drew her into his arms and kissed her, then eased her onto the bed and stretched out beside her. "Not until you've come at least three times." He tucked his finger under her bra cup and stroked her nipple. She wiggled her arms behind her and unfastened the garment, then peeled it away, revealing her naked breasts, nipples puckered and needy.

Kara moaned as his mouth covered her hard nipple. He licked the nub and she thought she might just come right now. His hand covered her other breast and the need in her built to an intolerable level.

"I want you inside me," she murmured.

"Not yet."

He sucked and she moaned, then he shifted to her other nipple and licked and sucked until she gasped. Then he kissed down her ribs to her belly, thrusting his tongue into her navel, then continuing down to her undies. He kissed along the lace top, then slowly rolled down the hem. He smiled as he stared at her dark curls, then drew her panties down her legs and off. He kissed up her thighs. She opened them as he moved upward, impatient to feel him . . . there. He paused and stared at her mound again, his hands stroking her inner thigh.

Finally, he leaned forward and his tongue touched her slit. She moaned loudly. His fingers slid along her moist opening, then he licked her length. She moaned again, then louder still as his tongue pressed against her clit. He dabbed and she flung her head from side to side. As he began to suck, she clung to his head. The heat, already so intense inside her, seemed to explode. She wailed as the orgasm claimed her.

He prowled over her and kissed her. When he tried to draw away, she wrapped her arms around him and dragged him to her, snaring his mouth again, her tongue diving inside. His undulated with hers and she arched her chest against him. His cock, hard and heavy, rested against her belly. She reached for it and stroked, loving the feel of his marble-hard flesh in her hands.

He stroked her breasts, then shifted downward and captured one of her nipples in his mouth, torturing her with intense pleasure as he sucked and licked first one, then the other nipple. She squeezed his cock and stroked up and down. So hard. So thick and long.

He sat up, his knees straddling her, and rested his hands over her stomach, then stroked upward . . . over her breasts . . . along her shoulders . . . past her neck to the crown of her head. He did that several times. Heat washed through her, and her incredible need heightened. Just as she was ready to beg him to impale her, he shifted and pressed his cockhead to her slick opening. He pressed forward, entering her slowly. She held her breath as his cockhead stretched her and then moved deeper as his thick shaft continued to fill her. He pushed forward until he impaled her fully. She gasped, wrapping her legs around him. He drew back slowly, then eased forward again, sending heat boiling within her. Back and forward again. His hard shaft stroked her insides and she melted around him. She clung to his shoulders, whimpering in pleasure as he began to thrust into her. Slow and steady, his long hard cock filling her each time. Her muscles clamped around him and intense pleasure washed through her. He slid back, then thrust forward again.

"Oh, God, I'm . . ."

He thrust deep.

"Yes!" Blissful sensations shimmered along her nerve endings and she gasped, then wailed as a blinding white light exploded within her. He kept thrusting and she cried out at the mind-shattering joy rippling through her.

It went on and on . . . as if she were lingering in heaven.

Slowly, she settled back to earth, still in his divine embrace.

She grinned at him. A silly, super-satisfied grin she couldn't seem to wipe from her face.

"That was . . . indescribable."

He chuckled and kissed her. "You think it's over?"

He stroked her clit and her eyes widened. His cock, still stretching her with its breadth and length, moved within her.

"Oh, God, I can't still . . ."

He drew back and thrust as he stroked her clit. She sucked in air as an orgasm welled in her again, explosive and earth-shattering. She clung to him as she rode the wave of interminable pleasure, his cock and finger stroking her to ever-growing heights.

She moaned, then sucked in air as the pleasure went on and on.

But his cock remained full and hard. She tightened her arms around his shoulders, wanting to share this with him more than she already was.

"Come . . . with me . . ." she implored.

He kissed her and smiled, then nodded. He groaned and, when she felt him release inside her, her orgasm rocked

into a higher gear. She clung to him as they climaxed together.

J.M. kissed Kara's cheek, loving the feel of her in his arms,
the contours of her soft body snuggled tightly against his.
They had dozed off together after their lovemaking.

"Would you like to go out somewhere for dinner or have
room service here?" He nuzzled her neck. "I prefer the latter,
so we can stay just like this. Naked and in bed together."

"Um . . . I should really get going."

She pushed back the covers, but he took her in his arms
and drew her against his body. His lips captured hers in a
persuasive kiss.

"Don't go yet." He smiled and kissed her neck again,
loving the soft sigh that escaped her lips. "You have to eat
sometime."

"I can . . . uh . . . grab something at the snack bar."

"Do you want to get away from me so badly?"

She gazed up at him. "No, of course not."

But he could see it in her eyes. She wanted to flee.
Clearly, she had feelings for him, but she seemed determined
to deny them. If he didn't do something about it, she'd
probably avoid him for the rest of the conference.

He couldn't let that happen.

He stroked her long dark hair back from her face and
tucked the strands behind her ear. Her skin, so soft under
his fingertips, made him want to glide his hands along her
shoulders, then over her satiny breasts. Even now, her nipples

hardened to beads and pressed into his chest in a most enticing way.

"Kara, this is the second time we've wound up in bed together in three days. Don't you think we should talk about it?"

"Talk?" Her brow furrowed and she shifted under him. "I don't think that right now . . ."

His cock slipped between her thighs, gliding over her slick opening, and she sighed. His cock swelled harder, wanting to slide into her. The panic in her eyes turned to glazed desire. She wanted him again as much as he wanted her.

Oh, God, he could barely contain himself. Her soft body beneath him. Tempting him. She drew in a deep breath, pressing her hard nipples into his chest. He pivoted his hips forward and she matched his movement.

He pressed his lips to her temple, then nipped her earlobe.

"Okay, so now isn't the time for talk." He positioned his cockhead at her opening, then dragged it the length of her slit. "You have a little time, though, don't you?"

She arched forward. "Yes. A little." Her husky, needy voice sent his senses sizzling.

He swirled his cockhead around her opening, watching her suck in a deep breath, then he slowly glided inside, burying himself in her hot depths.

He nibbled her neck, feeling her quickened pulse against his lips.

"You are so hot. So sexy."

He locked gazes with her as he drew back. Her wide sapphire eyes stared into his as he drove deep again. She moaned.

He hovered over her, propped up on his arms. "Oh, before we go too far."

"Hmm?"

He drew back, just short of the point where his cock would pull free, then stopped. "I do want to have that conversation with you." He shifted forward a little, embedding his cockhead inside her, but no more. She arched forward, but he shifted to deny her any more of his hard cock . . . then he smiled and glided forward, pressing deep into her. She moaned, and he pulled back again.

"Will you join me for dinner?" he asked.

She tightened her arms around his shoulders, pulling him forward. "Yes. Dinner."

He grinned, then drove deep into her. He felt her tighten around him, grasping his cock tightly in her warmth. He thrust. Deeper. Faster. She moaned and clung to him.

He watched her face as an orgasm encompassed her. The sheer beauty of her rapture made his heart swell. Ecstatic energy erupted through him, filling him with bliss at the same time that he climaxed inside her.

"So, you said you wanted to talk," Kara said.

J.M. pushed his drink aside and leaned toward her. "Ever since I first saw you, I've sensed something special between us, and I'd really like to explore that."

She fidgeted with her fork. "I thought we had been . . . exploring."

"I don't just mean something sexual." He took her hand. "Kara, I believe things happen for a reason. I also think we can influence what—and who—comes into our lives. I've been wanting someone special—a woman I could truly love—to come into my life. When I saw you . . ." He squeezed her hand. "I think there's real potential for a long-term relationship between us."

"A long-term relationship? But we hardly even know each other. And you're basing this on something like . . . what? That book *The Secret,* where people make something happen just by thinking about it?" She stared at him, dumbfounded. "You don't even know where I live. To decide right now to commit to a long-distance relationship, which is hard at the best of times, doesn't make any sense."

"You live in White Haven—I saw it on your luggage tag—and I'm only about fifty miles from there, in Spring Falls. That's not too far away."

She shook her head, but before she could utter a word, he jumped in again.

"Right now, I'm just asking that you give *us* a chance. That while we're here at the conference, you allow us to continue what we've started, then see how we feel at the end of the week." He took her hand. "I'm not asking you to make a long-term commitment right this second. Just to give us a chance to see where this goes."

"Look, J.M., it's true that there's a strong attraction between us, but . . . you and I are so different. We believe in different things. You believe in Tantra and . . . other stuff like that. I'm not really into the whole"—she waved her hands—"making things happen from . . . I don't know what you call it . . . a universal force?"

"We don't have to believe in the same things."

"But what about Tantra? That's a big part of your life. How can you become seriously involved with someone who doesn't believe in that?"

"Well, you still have a lot to learn for that article of yours. I might still win you over to Tantra yet."

"Don't bet on it." She pursed her lips and leaned toward him. "Why are you even asking me this? Why not just play it by ear and see what happens?"

"Because so far in our short relationship, I've gotten the impression you're a runner. You tried flirting with me, but as soon as you found we were together on the same plane, you panicked. Then when we had to land, you were afraid I'd ask you to spend the night with me."

She shifted in her chair. She didn't even bother to deny it. Damn, how could this man read her so well?

"As I recall, *I* asked *you*," she said.

"True, but that wasn't your first reaction. It does show, however, that when you decided to take a chance and go for it, things worked out very well." He smiled and stroked her hand. "You did enjoy that night, right?"

She drew in a deep breath and nodded. "It was spectacular."

"So, I'm just asking that you continue taking a chance.

Maybe things will work out better than either of us has ever dreamed. What have you got to lose?"

She compressed her lips. "We could crash and burn."

He shrugged. "We wouldn't be any worse off than if we hadn't tried. I think it's worth the gamble."

She studied him for a moment. His intense chocolate eyes stared into hers as he waited for her answer. He hoped they'd wind up as a couple. He wanted a long-term relationship. Happiness. *Love.*

"That first night we spent together . . . You asked me about love at first sight." She hesitated. "Why did you ask that? Do you think you're in love with me?"

He shrugged. "We both know it's too soon to know if we're in love, but I believe we are meant to fall in love."

Alarm bells blared in her head and she wanted to turn him down flat, then flee to her room.

Damn, he'd pegged her as a runner. And maybe he was right.

But she wasn't going to flee this time. She'd give it to him straight.

"I don't believe in love."

His dark eyes turned serious as he stared deeply into hers.

"Then what do you believe in, Kara?"

Nine

"I believe in hard work and perseverance. I don't believe there's a magic spell called love that will carry you through any difficulty that comes along. That's why there are so many divorces. Couples blame their problems on a lack of love. I blame it on false expectations and a lack of responsibility. I don't believe happiness is handed to you by some magical force we can't see or touch. I believe we make our own happiness."

"You know, what we believe in isn't really all that different." He smiled. "Come on, Kara. Give us a chance."

She knew she should just say no. Walk away now. But Grace's words returned to haunt her.

She hesitated. At Grace's workshop, Kara had learned that she'd been sabotaging her relationships. She gravitated to men who left her feeling lukewarm because they couldn't hurt her.

She might not believe in love, but that didn't mean she didn't believe in commitment and finding a happy, long-term relationship with a man. Marriage . . . children . . . growing old together . . . she wanted the whole package. And it made sense that when choosing a partner, she should look for someone with whom she felt a strong connection.

She had no guarantees that this thing with J.M. would last, despite the chemistry between them, but this week could give her an opportunity to do more than observe Tantra. It could also give her an opportunity to observe herself and pay attention to how she acted in a relationship—a relationship with someone who made her feel something for a change. Maybe that would give her some clue as to how she could grow past her issues and find a solid relationship in the future.

"I have serious doubts that this will lead anywhere, but I still need to do some research for my article. Spending time with you . . . dating you . . . would allow me to see how someone incorporates Tantra into their relationships. I just don't want to get your hopes up by making you think this might actually lead to something long-term."

"I'm a big boy. I can handle whatever happens."

"Can you really promise me that at the end of the week if I say I don't want to continue our relationship, that you'll just walk away? No guilt? No trying to change my mind?"

"I promise."

"Okay." She smiled. "I think I'm in for an exciting week."

Kara thought she heard a knock on the door, so she turned off the hair dryer. A knock sounded again. She laid the dryer on the vanity counter and walked to the door, then pulled it open.

Grace smiled at her. "Hi, Kara. Are you going to the party tonight? I thought we could go down together."

"Sure. I just have to fix my makeup. Come on in."

Ten minutes later, they stepped off the elevator on the second floor and headed to the large Orchid Ballroom. A redheaded woman, whose name was Connie according to her conference badge, sat at a table outside the room.

She smiled at them. "May I see your conference badges, please?"

Kara pulled hers out of her small purse and showed it to the woman. Grace flashed her badge, too. Connie found their names on her list, then crossed them off and handed them each two blue tickets and a red one.

"The red one's for a door prize and the blue ones are for drinks from the bar. Have fun."

Kara tucked two of her tickets into her purse, keeping a blue one in her hand.

"I'm going for a drink. Want one?" Kara asked. After her discussion with J.M. over dinner, she could really use a drink.

"Sure thing."

They stood in line, then Kara ordered a Sex on the Beach because it just seemed so appropriate. Grace followed suit.

Kara took a sip of her cocktail as they walked past the people milling around the bar. The lights were low and a D.J. played music, but people could still hear each other talk.

Grace glanced around. "I was really hoping to see my friend Jeremy. I had hoped to catch him for dinner, but he didn't answer his phone."

So Grace had been the one who'd called while she and J.M. had been . . . busy.

"I'd really like you to meet him," Grace continued.

Grace must have forgotten about Kara's interview with him today.

Kara turned to her. "About that, Grace, I—"

"Hello there."

That deep voice of velvet sent tingles down her spine. She turned around and there stood J.M.

"Jeremy. Great! This is my friend Kara and . . ." Grace glanced from Kara's face to J.M.'s broad grin. "You two know each other?"

Kara wasn't sure how Grace had figured it out. Maybe from Kara's flushed cheeks or the way J.M.'s gaze lingered on her with a maddeningly satisfied expression.

"This is the woman from the airport." J.M. sipped his drink.

"Really?" Grace sent a bemused glance Kara's way.

That was odd, because from what Grace had told her at lunch today, she hadn't connected with J.M. yet . . . and she certainly hadn't had time since then because Kara had kept him pretty busy. How could J.M. have told Grace about her?

"There's a free table over there," J.M. said. "Why don't you two sit and I'll get us another round?"

Kara glanced at her half-empty glass. "I'm okay."

"We're having Sex on the Beach."

He smiled. "Okay, then. I'll be right back."

Kara and Grace walked to the table and settled in.

"So what did he tell you about me?" Kara asked. "And when?"

"We were talking on the phone when he was at the airport, and he told me he thought you . . . would hit it off."

There was something Grace wasn't saying. Oh, God, did she know about their one-night stand?

J.M. returned and placed three drinks on the table. He sat down beside Kara and rested his arm on the back of her chair. Grace noticed but said nothing. As his fingers played along Kara's shoulder, heat shimmered through her. Memories of the intensity of her arousal when he'd explained the energy of Tantra, his hands lingering over her, washed through her.

"When did you two meet?" J.M. asked.

"I'm just across the hall from Kara. We met on our way to registration. This is who I had dinner with the first night."

He smiled at Kara. "So we almost ran into each other again last night."

"Did Kara tell you what she does for a living?" Grace's eyes met Kara's and she gave her a wink. "She's a sex columnist."

"Has she happened to tell you her opinion of Tantra?" J.M. asked.

His hand stroked lightly across her shoulder, sending tremors through her.

"Well, I got the idea she's not really into it. I told her at dinner last night that I thought you could change her mind."

He smiled. "I think I'm starting to make some headway on that."

Kara's shoulders slumped. She wasn't sure what to say. She finished her drink and pushed away the empty glass. J.M. slid the full one in front of her.

"Kara, did you tell Jeremy your concerns about your column? He might have some ideas for you."

J.M. turned to her. "What concerns?"

"It's nothing, really."

"She's afraid her editor thinks her column is getting stale. She could use some fresh ideas."

Kara shrugged and took a sip of her drink.

"A sex column." J.M. swirled his drink, considering. "There are a lot of interesting topics, but you're looking for something a little different. Something fresh."

She took another drink. Her head felt a little fuzzy. She wasn't used to drinking much. "I've done orgasms and dating techniques, how to know if a guy is into you—stuff like that. I'm doing an article on flirting."

"Really?"

At his amused expression, she pursed her lips and took another sip.

"One of the workshops is about women's sexual fantasies. Have you done anything like that?" Grace asked.

"You mean being rescued by a knight in shining armor—that sort of thing?" Kara asked.

"I was thinking more about bondage, sex in an elevator . . . threesomes," Grace responded.

Kara felt her cheeks flush. "I . . . uh . . . wouldn't really know about that kind of thing."

"Now, I could definitely help you with that," J.M. said.

"You want to have sex in an elevator?" she blurted before her brain censor could kick in.

"Well, of course. But I was thinking I could help you identify various types of fantasies. I've researched women's fantasies as part of what I do. I had a friend who used hypnotism to discover what her deepest fantasies were, and to bring them to life. She'd always had a problem coming to orgasm and it helped her immensely. Doing a column about fantasies could be very helpful and informative for your readers."

"So . . . you're offering to hypnotize me?"

"I could do that. Or . . . maybe I could arrange something a little more interesting."

After the party, J.M. walked Kara and Grace to their floor. Intense awareness of J.M. rippled through her as she'd stood beside him in the elevator and now as they walked down the hall. They stopped in front of Kara's door.

"Well, I'm heading off to bed. Good night." Grace unlocked her door and went inside.

Kara glanced at J.M., ready to tell him she needed to get some sleep, that she'd see him the next morning, but he rested his hands on her shoulders and gazed at her with simmering chocolate brown eyes. Heat emanated from his hands, washing through her, turning her insides to mush. An incredible yearning jolted through her. She stepped closer, rested her hand on his cheek, and kissed him. His arms came around her and he tugged her tight to his body. Their lips joined in a blaze of passion.

Their lips parted and she gazed into his eyes.

"Come in," she murmured breathlessly.

She reached into her small purse and pulled out her key card. As soon as they were inside the room, he shoved the door closed and tugged her into his arms again, then plundered her mouth with sure strokes of his tongue. She thrust her tongue into his mouth, which tasted of rye.

She fumbled with her blouse and dropped it from her body, then unfastened her skirt. His shirt fell to the floor, then his pants. As she gazed at the huge erection stretching his charcoal briefs, she felt a raging need build inside her. Hormones spiraled through her in a chaotic dance and her insides ached with need. She shed her skirt and panty hose, then stroked her finger over his bulge.

"None of that Tantra stuff tonight," she insisted. "I want hot and heavy." She stripped off her bra and cupped her hands over her breasts. "I don't want you to hold back."

She tweaked her nipples, pinching them until they nearly burst with pleasure.

His eyes burned with lust as her hands stroked her breasts. When he still didn't make a move toward her, she slid her fingers into her panties and slipped them inside.

"I'm wet. Really, really wet. Thinking of you."

She slid her panties down her legs and kicked them away, her yearning for him gnawing at her.

"I want you to take me like a wild man. Show me how much you want me."

As she continued to stroke herself, his eyes grew dark. She felt naughty and . . . intensely sexy. He stepped toward her, a powerful, almost dangerous aura about him. He wrapped his hands around her hips, then glided them over her butt. He pulled her tight to his body, then slid his hands under her thighs and lifted her up. She wrapped her arms and legs around him. His cock pressed against her wet slit, only the thin cotton of his briefs between them.

His mouth captured hers, his tongue delving deep inside. Overwhelmed by his intense masculinity, she barely noticed them moving across the room until her back thumped against the wall. He pressed his body tight against hers, then worked his hard cock free of its cotton prison. His thick cockhead stroked her slit.

His tongue thrust deep into her mouth and his body drove forward, thrusting his rock-hard cock deep inside her. She whimpered at the searing pleasure of his shaft filling her so completely . . . and so suddenly.

"Yes," she breathed into his ear. "Take me!"

His gaze locked on hers and he drew back and thrust into her again. Her eyelids fluttered closed . . . briefly . . . then opened to his compelling dark gaze.

"Kara, look at me while I'm fucking you."

Excitement raced through her at his coarse language.

Opal Carew

His body held her pressed hard to the wall, his cock impaling her like a stake holding her in place.

"That's what you want me to do, right? Fuck you."

She nodded. "Yes."

He pivoted his pelvis, pushing his cock deeper.

"Fast and hard."

"Oh, yes."

He drew back and thrust again. Pleasure catapulted through her. He rammed into her again and again.

"Yes. Oh, please . . ."

Joy vibrated through her as he thrust into her like a jack-hammer.

"Make me come," she pleaded, clinging to his shoulders.

He grasped her knees and lifted them, opening her legs wider, driving his cock impossibly deep as he rammed her against the wall with every thrust. She moaned.

He leaned in and nipped her neck.

"Am I making you come?"

She nodded, whimpering as intoxicating bliss filled her . . . then white-hot sensation blazed through her, erupting in a fierce explosion of ecstasy.

She collapsed against him, gasping for air. The whole experience had been so . . . intense and . . . erotic.

He carried her to the bed, his cock still immersed in her, and laid her down. He kissed her tenderly, then began to glide his cock in and out. She moaned as the pleasure flared again.

"You are incredibly sexy, sweetheart."

He stroked her clit with his finger and she cried out in

102

pleasure. His cock stroked her with slow, deep thrusts, while he flicked her clit. She clutched him tight to her body as another orgasm swept through her.

"Oh, yes . . . yes . . ." She gasped.

Still he glided his cock into her, then did a little spiral. Her orgasm intensified, then hot, searing joy blazed through her.

Finally, she slumped back on the bed.

He smiled as he stroked her hair tenderly. "I see you're really into this fantasy idea."

"Fantasy?"

"You wanted me to be a bad-boy type and take you. That's a fantasy of sorts. And a very effective one, it seems."

"It was pretty great."

He stood up and pulled her to her feet, then kissed her thoroughly.

"Do you want to . . . stay the night?" She liked the idea of him in her bed. Snuggling all night long.

"Absolutely."

She slid under the covers and he curled in behind her. His erection glided between her legs as he cupped her breast.

"You didn't come," she said.

"With you writhing in pleasure in my arms? Are you kidding? Of course I came. I just didn't release."

"Oh."

She couldn't really argue with him. And she liked his long, hard cock nestled between her legs. Pressing against her slit. She wiggled a little closer and tremors of pleasure rippled through her. Of course, she might never get to sleep.

But the warmth of his body pressed against hers, combined with the afterglow of their lovemaking, quickly lulled her into a contented sleepiness.

He nuzzled her ear. "What if tomorrow we fulfill another fantasy?"

"Mmm. That would be nice," she said as she drifted closer to sleep.

"What about sex with a stranger?"

"Mm hmm. That's a good idea."

Ten

The sound of her alarm dragged Kara from sleep. She tapped the snooze button, then sank back against J.M.'s warm body.

"Do you have to get up right away?" He nuzzled her neck.

"I have a few minutes to spare." She rolled around and faced him with a smile.

"Good." He brushed her lips with his. She wrapped her arms around him and deepened the kiss. His hard cock pressed against her belly. His hand slid between them and . . . his cock slid inside her. Then he pulled her close and cuddled her.

And cuddled her.

After another few moments, she wiggled a little, enjoying the feel of his stiff shaft moving inside her

She stroked her hand across his broad chest, enjoying the ripples of muscle beneath her fingertips. "Aren't you going anywhere with this?" she asked.

"Actually, I just wanted to enjoy the closeness and intimacy." He kissed her temple. "In Tantra, the goal isn't orgasm."

"Screw that," she said, tipping him onto his back and trapping him between her knees. She grinned impishly. "*I want an orgasm.*"

She lifted her body, then pushed herself down on him again. His hard cock stroked her inner walls, sending ripples of pleasure through her. She took his hands and placed them on her breasts, then pushed herself up and sank back down on him. When he twitched inside her, she smiled.

He leaned forward and nipped her nipple with a light brush of his teeth, then sucked. She dropped her head back, moaning softly, as his hand slid down her stomach and his fingertip stroked over her clit. High-voltage sensations sparked through her. She increased her rhythm, pleasure building in her. He sucked her nipple while he toyed with her clit. His cock glided up and down her passage. She squeezed him inside, intensifying the sensation. He cupped her buttocks and pressed together, squeezing him inside her. She sucked in air as the blissful onset of orgasm swept through her . . . then exploded in fiery sparks of ecstasy. She moaned long and loud as she ground her pelvis against him. He flipped her under him and drove deep. She gasped as another orgasm erupted inside her. He swirled and thrust. The wave of ecstasy swept through her . . . on and on.

Finally, she slumped back on the bed and smiled up at him.

"Now that's what I call an orgasm."

———

Kara stroked her soapy hands across J.M.'s back as the warm shower water streamed over them. He turned around to face her.

"Do you want me to arrange that fantasy for tonight?"

She grabbed the bar of soap and lathered up her hands again, then dragged them over his hard, sculpted abs, then down the fur on his belly.

"What fantasy?" she asked.

"Sex with a stranger. Remember? I suggested it last night. As research for a column on women's sexual fantasies."

She vaguely remembered him mentioning something about it as she fell asleep last night. As she stroked over his groin, his cock hardened and swelled. She wrapped her hands around his cock and soaped it thoroughly.

"I already did the sex with a stranger. You and I two nights ago. Remember?"

He lathered up his hands and ran his soapy fingers over her breasts. The nipples puckered.

"What I'm talking about is totally anonymous sex. When you don't even know who it is who is making love to you. Not what he looks like, what his name is. Nothing."

"How could I not know what he looks like if I'm making love with him?"

"A blindfold."

She smiled. "Really. That sounds fun. So you'll pretend to be a total stranger?"

"Who said anything about pretending?"

She stepped back and stared at him wide-eyed. "You

want me to make love to a complete stranger? Someone I know nothing about?"

"That's right. It's a fantasy about sex *with a stranger.*"

She sucked in a deep breath. "I can't do that." She shook her head. "And if I could, I wouldn't know . . . I mean, he could be anyone. I could pass him the next day and not even know it."

"Exactly."

He turned her around and pressed his body close to hers.

"Just imagine. He comes up behind you . . ." His hands stroked along her sides. "You can't see him, but you feel his breath on your neck." His hands slid over her breasts. "On your body." He pressed his pelvis against her, his cock pushing against her buttocks.

She imagined he was a stranger. Touching her. Stroking her. When he pressed his cock to her slick opening and pushed inside, she moaned. She rested her hands against the tile wall of the shower as he pulled her snug to his body, his arms gripping her tightly, and thrust into her. A stranger, making love to her. After a few short strokes, intense pleasure rocketed through and she gasped in orgasm.

She slumped in his arms, reveling in the sexy heat of residual pleasure.

"You wouldn't even know at first if it was really a stranger or not."

"So it could be you pretending?"

"It could be. . . . Does that help you decide? Not knowing?"

"I don't know. It makes it sexy."

He turned her around and kissed her. "Doesn't it make it even sexier knowing it will more likely be real?"

She stared into his dark espresso-brown eyes and nodded. "Yes, I guess it does."

"It's wild," Kara said as she faced Grace over the lunch table. "J.M. and I have been talking about acting out a sexual fantasy for my column, but I don't think he means it to be an act."

All the tables in the hotel restaurant were full, mostly with conference attendees trying to get lunch as quickly as possible and get back in time for the afternoon sessions. The sound of chatting voices and cutlery clinking against chinaware resounded. A waitress zipped past Kara and Grace to deliver food to the next table.

"Oh? What's the fantasy?" Grace jabbed her fork into a chunk of chicken on her lunch salad, then popped it in her mouth.

"Sex with an anonymous stranger."

Grace put down her fork and stared at Kara. "Really? That's pretty adventurous. So you've agreed to do it?"

"Well, the thing is, I'm not sure if it will be J.M. acting as a stranger—I'd have a blindfold on—or whether he really intends to bring in a stranger."

Kara took a spoonful of the delicious minestrone soup.

"What did he say exactly?"

"He said that I wouldn't know at first if it was a stranger

or not. He seems to want to make it more exciting by keeping me uncertain."

Grace tapped her fingers on the tabletop. "But he did warn you it could be an actual stranger?"

"That's right. When I said it could be sexy not knowing for sure, he asked if it wasn't even sexier knowing it probably will be real."

A waitress stopped by their table with a water jug dripping with condensation and refilled their glasses, the ice tinkling against the glass as she poured. Kara took her last bite of salad and the waitress took her empty plate away.

Kara leaned back in her chair. "Well, all I can say is, make sure you're okay with it *really* being a stranger, because he's clearly given you fair warning."

"I know. Maybe I should just tell him I can't go through with it." Kara took a sip of her ice water.

"That's up to you, but just so you know, I've been friends with J.M. a long time. He's someone you can depend on. I trust his judgment. If you feel you can, too, then you can trust that he'll pick someone who is discreet . . . someone he would trust with your welfare . . . and probably someone who's sexy as hell. It sounds like an exciting opportunity to me."

Excitement quivered through her at Grace's words. She was right. J.M. would be careful whom he chose. It wouldn't be like a real stranger whom she knew nothing about. She would know that J.M. trusted him.

And anyway, it would probably just be J.M. pretending.

Bliss

"I'm helping a woman friend explore some possibilities . . . specifically, sexual fantasies," J.M. said as Quinn tipped back his beer. The lunch break would be over soon and they'd have to return to the conference for the afternoon sessions. He couldn't put off asking any longer.

Quinn placed his glass on the table.

"Really? Sounds like fun. Is this your girlfriend's sister?"

"Ex-girlfriend's sister and . . . no. I told you, I'm not going to get sexually involved with Grace." J.M. took one of the tangy chicken wings from the basket in front of them and took a bite, then washed it down with a sip of beer. "Listen, have you been tested recently?"

"Tested?" Quinn took a sip of his beer. "Oh, you mean . . . yeah, sure. Always before I come to a conference like this." He narrowed his eyes. "Why? You're not suggesting you and I . . . ? 'Cause I'm totally into women."

"No, nothing like that. I was actually wondering if you might be interested in helping out. With the fantasies."

Quinn's face split in a broad grin. "Are you kidding?" He leaned forward. "You're not talking about me just being a cameraman or some such?"

"The scenario is sex with a stranger. Anonymous, so we'll go with a blindfold for her. She doesn't know you, so you'll be the main player."

Quinn's eyebrows quirked. "Since she'll have a blindfold, you could play the role yourself. Why share?"

"You know I'm a purist. It's not the same if it's not really a stranger. I think she deserves the full experience."

Quinn chuckled. "Okay, then." He clinked his glass beer mug against J.M.'s. "I take it you're not one to feel threatened by a second man being with your woman."

If only you knew. All morning, J.M. had fought the niggling jealousy he felt at the thought of Quinn touching Kara . . . making love to Kara. He had almost backed out in favor of playing the role himself. At the same time, he got incredibly turned on thinking about how much pleasure Kara would experience by acting out this fantasy.

And the increased adrenaline blasting through her system when she finally realized it really was a stranger gliding his cock into her would shoot her to astonishing heights of ecstasy.

In fact, now that he'd set it up with Quinn, it would be sheer torture waiting for this evening to come.

Kara stepped into J.M.'s room, one hand clasped around the other.

"I've got to admit that I'm . . . a little nervous," she said.

J.M. closed the door, then stepped toward her and stroked her hair behind her ear. The gentle touch sent tingles along her neck.

"You've got nothing to be worried about."

She'd been thinking of this all day. Anticipating, yet uncertain. Unsure she actually wanted to go through with it.

Which was silly because most likely it would be J.M. pretending to be the stranger. He wouldn't really bring another man in here to be with her.

Would he?

And if he did, would she really let a strange man touch her? Make love to her?

Of course, since she'd be blindfolded, she wouldn't know for sure whether it was J.M. or someone else until it was too late to back out.

A quiver began deep in her stomach at the thought of being with a stranger whom she couldn't see. Not knowing if it even was a stranger.

J.M. stepped back and eyed her outfit. "Good choice."

His frank, masculine appreciation made her feel sexy. He'd asked her to wear a sundress with a short hemline. She'd chosen a black dress with a pattern of large tropical flowers, but she was certain it wasn't the fabric he admired as his gaze drifted down the deep V neckline. It was a halter top, fitted to the waist with a full but very short skirt.

"Turn around for me."

She turned and he chuckled.

"The tie closure at the back of the neck is a nice touch."

He touched the tie and for a moment, she thought he was going to unfasten it, but his fingertips trailed down her bare spine. He flattened his hand on her back and drew her around to face him, then into his arms. She gazed at him as his lips approached hers, then she tipped up her head and their mouths joined. With his arms around her and his lips moving on hers, she felt her anxiety slip away. His masculine presence held her full attention. His hard, broad chest . . . his strong, muscular arms . . . his full, sexy lips. And his tongue sweeping into her mouth as if claiming it.

She sighed and melted against him. He released her lips, then took her hand and led her into the bedroom.

The first thing she noticed was a silver pole on one side of the room.

"What is that?"

"It's a pole."

"I can see that. You had a pole installed in your hotel room?"

"It's a friction-fit pole. Totally portable and won't leave a mark."

She sent it a leery glance. "Are you planning on having a stripper in later? Because I'm not planning on dancing."

He laughed. "Don't worry. You'll find out what it's for soon enough."

She pursed her lips and nodded. "Okay then."

He drew her farther into the room toward the bed. He sat down and drew her into a standing position in front of him.

On the bedside table, she saw a strip of black cloth.

The blindfold.

He wrapped his hands around her waist, then slid them downward, over her hips, past the short hem of her skirt to midthigh . . . then up to her hem, which he toyed with. She dragged her gaze from the blindfold to his simmering espresso eyes.

"Lift your skirt for me so I can see what's underneath."

She reached for the hem of her skirt and lifted the light fabric to show him her black panties.

"Very pretty."

His hands glided around behind her and stroked over the

silky fabric covering her buttocks. He circled around to the front, then caressed the front of her panties. Her eyelids fell closed as she enjoyed his gentle touch. Then he tugged on the elastic waistband and pulled the panties down her thighs, past her calves, then dropped them to her feet. She opened her eyes and saw his chocolate gaze fixed on her dark curls.

She felt incredibly exposed and . . . very turned on. His frank, male scrutiny sent tingles rushing through her insides. She wanted him to touch her . . . to slide his fingers inside her. To lick her and tease her, then bring her to an intense orgasm.

She had to stop herself from widening her stance to offer him easy access.

He took her right hand and drew it from the fabric of her skirt, which she still held in the air. She realized she was still holding up her hem with her other hand, so she released it. Her skirt fell back into place, covering her naked mound, but she still felt exposed. She wondered if he would place her hand between her legs and encourage her to stimulate herself. She felt the moisture collect inside her, waiting for his discovery.

Instead, he kissed the back of her hand, then turned it over and pressed his mouth to her palm in a gentle caress. Then he reached to the bedside table and picked up the blindfold.

"Are you ready?" he asked.

Eleven

"Um . . ." Kara's heart thumped in her chest. She wasn't at all sure she was ready.

J.M. grinned. "I just mean for the blindfold. Don't worry, we're not going to move that fast. Your close encounter won't happen immediately. I want you to get used to the blindfold first."

She nodded. He patted the bed beside him and she sat down, then he placed the blindfold over her eyes and tied it behind her head. Snug, but not too tight.

"Okay?" he asked.

She nodded. "Um . . . shouldn't we have a safe word or something?"

He laughed. "It won't be necessary. If you say you want to stop, we stop. It's as simple as that. If we were tying you up or doing a scenario where we captured you and pretended to take you against your will, then we'd have a safe word."

The thought of that sent quivers through her. Being

overpowered by J.M. or . . . *and* . . . a stranger. She couldn't believe how turned on that made her.

"I have recorded something for you to listen to. I know hypnotherapy, so first I have an introduction to relax you, called an induction, then I'll walk you through a scenario to set the scene."

"And you did it as a recording so I wouldn't hear where your voice is coming from . . . so I won't know if the man I'm with is you or . . . someone else."

"Actually, I recorded it so it will become more like your own voice in your head . . . so it would be less intrusive."

She nodded. Soft music began to play and his voice spoke softly, telling her to breathe deeply.

His voice and the music relaxed her. His hand rested on her shoulders and he walked her across the room. He took her hands and guided them forward until they came in contact with cold metal. The dance pole. He wrapped her hands around it, then moved away. She wasn't sure how far.

"Now, imagine you are in total darkness," his recorded voice said. "You are on a subway train between stops. The train has stopped. An electrical failure. The train is very crowded and there are people all around you. Hang on to the pole in case the train starts up again suddenly."

She tightened her hands around the cold metal pole, gripping it snugly.

"Before the train stopped, you were aware of a handsome stranger on the train near you. You didn't get a good look at him—you hadn't wanted to stare—but you can feel him close by."

She felt the heat of a body close to her . . . or was that just her imagination stimulated by J.M.'s words? Was J.M. standing just behind her?

"You know there are people around, but no one can see anything. It is strangely liberating. You could strip off your dress entirely and no one would know. You could glide your fingers under your dress . . . where you are totally naked . . . and slide them inside. You could come to orgasm without anyone knowing."

Was he going to tell her to do that? She knew she would follow his words, whatever he told her to do.

"The handsome stranger is behind you. You can feel him. You don't know how close, but are intensely aware of his heat."

The hairs on the back of her neck stood up.

"Your legs are becoming stiff, standing so still. You shift a little."

She followed his instructions, shuffling a little, and stifled a gasp as she bumped into a hard body.

"His arm catches you around the waist so you don't tumble."

A strong arm encircled her body and she landed against a hard torso.

It was J.M.

At least, she was pretty sure it was J.M.

"You like his touch. You like feeling his arm around you in this utter darkness. His other arm slides around your waist and you lean against him."

The man's other arm—J.M.'s arm—encircled her. He drew her against his body. Hot and hard. He stepped closer, pressing her against the pole, which she still gripped tightly.

"This total stranger is pressed tight against you. You don't know him . . . he doesn't know you . . . but you want him to touch you. You are aching for him to touch you."

Oh, God, *she wanted* him to touch her.

J.M.

Or the stranger.

"His hand strokes over your hip."

The man's—the *stranger's*—hand glided over her buttocks. She tingled all over.

The soft, calming music continued playing, but J.M.'s voice did not. The man's face pressed against her hair and he breathed her in, then nuzzled her neck. Was he a little shorter than J.M.? Maybe an inch?

Oh, God, this couldn't really be a stranger?

The thought sent tremors through her. Did she really want it to be a stranger?

His hand stroked over her shoulder, then down the front of her dress, caressing lightly over one breast before settling on her waist. He drew her back against him. She could feel a large bulge against her backside.

He was clearly as turned on as she was.

He pressed her forward, more tightly against the pole. It pressed between her breasts . . . and her thighs. He stroked around her waist, then down her buttocks. Not quite ready for him to steal under her dress, she arched forward. The cold steel pushed against her mound. She felt the fabric of her dress slip away—he was tugging it upward—and the cold metal pushed against her hot, wet opening.

The hand behind her slid under her dress and cupped her buttock. His other hand slid around to her other buttock and he lifted her slightly, pushing her slit against the pole. Her vagina clenched in need and she pressed her knees together. He pivoted her hips forward until her clit rubbed against the metal. Her shoulders dropped back against him.

He kissed her neck, then shifted his hands around to her breasts, still encased in the cotton of her halter top, as he held her against the pole with his body. He cupped her breasts and massaged them in his hands. Different from how J.M. did. A little firmer in his grip. His fingers a little longer.

He nibbled her earlobe, whispers of his warm breath tickling her ear, driving her wild. He released her breasts, then she felt his hands behind her neck, and her top fell free. His hands cupped her once again. Warm, masculine hands on her naked flesh. Her nipples blossomed against his palms as he caressed her. She moaned.

One hand glided down her stomach and his body eased back, releasing her from the pole. He cupped her hot, wet mound and she arched against him . . . wanting . . . *needing* . . . the pressure of his hand. First one finger slid inside her, then another. He swirled around, then glided in and out. A third finger slid inside and he thrust a couple of times. She rested against his solid chest, allowing him to glide within her. His thumb found her clit and she gasped. With his other hand, he stroked up her neck, then his finger brushed her lips and glided into her mouth. She sucked on him, then he withdrew. A moment later, his wet finger stroked over her nipple, like a damp tongue licking her. So many sensations danced within her. She felt faint from pleasure.

She reached around behind her and stroked over that impressive bulge. She found his zipper and drew it down. She wanted to touch him. To hold his hard cock in her hand and stroke it. She reached inside and wrapped her hand around him.

Oh, God, this was not J.M. He was thicker . . . not quite as long. . . .

Tremors quivered through her belly . . . but she wanted him. She did *not* want to stop now.

She stroked her hand the length of him. His cock hardened even more . . . became like a hot steel rod. She released him and widened her legs, then arched forward against the pole, raising her derriere. He nuzzled her ear.

"You are one incredible turn-on," he murmured, low enough so the imaginary passengers wouldn't hear.

Not J.M.'s voice.

But she didn't care. He was her sexy stranger and she wanted him. *Bad.*

He cupped her buttocks with both hands, caressing her in circles. She angled her body forward more, bumping her ass against him. Taking the hint, he drew his hand from her ass, then slid it over her slick opening. His hand slid away and his cock pressed forward, dragging along her slit. She moaned at the feel of the hard flesh stimulating her. His cock glided along her several times, then his cockhead bumped against her opening, seeking entry. She leaned forward, changed the angle of her body more, inviting him in.

"Oh, doll, you are something else."

He pushed forward and his cockhead pressed into her a little at a time. She clung to the cold metal pole as his hot, stiff pole pushed deeper and deeper, stretching her.

Once he was fully immersed, he wrapped his hands around her hips and pulled her tight to him.

"No one in the subway is aware of what you're doing," J.M. said. There was no interruption in the music. He was really speaking now. And his voice sounded a little hoarse. No doubt he was turned on by the sight of the stranger taking her from behind.

The stranger drew back, his cockhead dragging on her inner passage, then glided forward again, filling her.

"There are people all around you. You can't see the stranger who is touching you . . . making love to you. He's just a hard body in the darkness. But in the magic of this moment, you can talk, or make sounds . . . and hear words . . . without anyone else being aware of anything but silence. You can tell him what you want."

"Tell me, gorgeous." He drew out, then thrust forward again. "What do you want?"

His hand stroked up her stomach, then brushed over her nipple. She moaned as the hard nub pulsed with pleasure. He squeezed it between his fingers.

She wanted to talk to him. "I want . . ." She didn't know what words to use.

He drove into her again and she pushed back to meet him.

"Kara, in the darkness, you can use whatever words you want."

She focused on J.M.'s soothing voice.

"No one will judge. No one will even know."

"I . . . want you to *fuck* me." The word felt strange coming from her mouth, but it felt erotic and . . . oh, God, so sexy. "I want you to drive into my *pussy* . . . fast . . . and hard."

"Oh, yeah, gorgeous."

He thrust forward, driving into her deep, pushing her tight against the pole. The hard metal squeezed against her clit and she tightened her thighs against the pole, squeezing the stranger's cock inside her, too.

She whimpered at the intense pleasure. He released her nipple and wrapped his arm around her and the pole, pulling her tighter against it, and cupped her other breast.

He thrust again. His hands wrapped around her hips. Every time he thrust into her, he pulled her tight to him.

"Would you like your nipples sucked?" the stranger asked. He thrust forward. Driving deep.

"Ohhh . . . yes . . . but . . ."

He thrust again.

"Don't . . . stop. . . ."

She almost jumped as she felt a mouth cover her nipple. J.M.

Oh, God, he was touching her, too . . . but only his mouth.

His tongue rolled her nipple around, then he sucked.

"Oh, God . . . yes."

123

Every nerve ending quivered with sensation.

The stranger drove his rock-hard cock into her again and J.M. teased and sucked on her nipple. Her fingers spiked through J.M.'s hair while her other hand continued to cling to the pole.

Intense pleasure pummeled through her with each thrust of the cock inside her. J.M. caressed her other breast as he sucked again and the pleasure intensified.

"I'm going to come, gorgeous. But I want you with me."

He thrust faster. J.M. sucked harder. Raging pleasure rippled through every part of her . . . then she burst into orgasm. He thrust forward again and liquid heat filled her.

She moaned, clinging to the pole as ecstasy pulsed through her.

Her handsome stranger drew her to a standing position and gave her a quick squeeze, then stepped back. His cock slipped from her body.

She'd just had an absolutely incredible orgasm . . . but she wanted more. Somewhere along the way, J.M. had released her breast. She reached out for him and clutched a handful of shirt. She pulled him toward her, then found his face and drew it to hers. As soon as their lips touched, his arms tugged her against him, his mouth plundering hers, his tongue delving into her. She stroked down his chest and fumbled with his jeans, quickly releasing his hard cock. She stroked him.

"Fuck me, J.M."

"Oh, God, Kara."

She guided his cock to her wet opening and eased it inside. He pulled her against him, driving his cock into her.

She wrapped her legs around him, then felt the metal pole at her back as he used it to steady her.

"Fuck me fuck me fuck me!" she cried.

He drove into her again . . . and again. Immediately, another orgasm washed through her.

"Come inside me. Just like the stranger did."

To her complete satisfaction, she felt his cock release inside her, the hot semen filling her with pleasure.

She squeezed her legs tightly around him, as if pulling him deeper would give her more of him.

"Ohhh . . . Yes!"

The intense joy washing through her heightened . . . then slowly ebbed, leaving her sated and . . . exultant.

J.M. captured her mouth again in a passionate kiss, then he scooped her into his arms and carried her across the room. He eased her down onto the bed. She felt his fingers at the back of her head, then the blindfold released. She glanced around quickly, but saw no sign of the stranger.

"He's gone."

J.M. tugged down the zipper of her dress—the top already hung at her waist. She arched upward to allow him to pull the garment down and off. She climbed into bed as he shed his clothes, then he climbed in beside her.

"It really was a stranger," she murmured, gazing into his simmering brown eyes.

He smiled. "Of course. But you knew that even before he touched you."

She nodded. He drew her into his arms and she snuggled against him.

"You know, I tend to forget that I'm a little more free about sex than most people. I hope that wasn't too much for you."

"Not at all."

"Any regrets?" he asked.

All kinds of negative voices rippled through her mind, but she pushed them aside. What they'd just done was sex between consenting adults. Playing out a fantasy. It was wild and sexy. She always encouraged her readers to push their boundaries and follow their bliss. Why shouldn't she?

"No regrets. That was a truly incredible experience." She kissed J.M., stroking his lips with hers. "Thank you for making it happen."

He caressed her cheek tenderly. "Thank you for letting me be a part of it."

She sighed in his embrace, loving the feel of his strong arms around her, and gave herself over to sleep.

After the morning sessions, Kara went to the lobby and sat down in one of the plush chairs in the reception area to wait for J.M. so they could go to lunch. She spotted him walking toward her from the escalator. A smile curled his lips when he saw her and warmth filled her at the sight.

She stood up and walked toward him.

"Hi," he said. "I talked to Grace this morning, and she's going to join us for lunch. Grace suggested a restaurant already. That okay with you?"

"Sure. I take it it's not the one in the hotel, so I'd better go get my coat."

"Actually, good news. Grace discovered there's a sky-walk right from the hotel to a whole shopping center, and there are a number of sit-down restaurants. No need to brave the snow."

"Great. Lead on."

She linked her arm with his and followed him to a special elevator. After a short ride up, they walked down a hall, then across a skywalk over the street. A moment later, they stepped into a large shopping mall.

"Over this way," J.M. said. "It's called the Black Swan."

She followed him past several clothing boutiques, a jewelry store with glittering diamond rings and gold chains in the window, and a store with an eclectic mix of household decor items.

"There it is." He pointed at a place with darkened windows and a heavy wooden door with a stained-glass inset.

He opened the door for her and she stepped inside. A huddle of people filled the entryway.

"It looks like a line." She glanced at her watch. They had only an hour before the afternoon sessions began. "I wonder if we'll have time."

"Grace said she'd get here early to grab a table. Wait here while I go check."

She nodded and stepped to the side as she watched J.M. disappear into the crowd. As she waited, watching the hostess pick up some menus and lead three people away, a familiar voice sent a tingle down her spine.

Her sexy anonymous stranger.

Twelve

Kara tilted her head, but couldn't detect it again. . . . Wait, there it was. She couldn't make out the words, but it was definitely the man from last night.

"I found them." J.M.'s voice, and his touch on her arm, startled her. "What's wrong? You look like you've seen a ghost."

"I . . . uh . . . I think I heard . . . someone I know." She didn't want to tell him she thought she'd heard the man who'd made love to her last night. Although she didn't know anything about him, even what he looked like, J.M. obviously did. Would he feel he had to introduce them? She did *not* want that to happen.

"Do you want to find your friend and invite her to join us?" J.M. asked.

"No. Don't worry about it."

"Okay. The hostess said Grace is already here so she'll take us to the table."

He rested his hand on the small of her back and guided

her through the crowd. The hostess returned after seating another two people and smiled.

"Ready?" She led them around a corner to a table near the front window.

"Hi, Kara. J.M." Grace said. "As you can see, J.M., I ran into a friend of yours."

Beside Grace sat a tall, handsome guy with straight, light brown hair, cut short on the sides and longer on top, with errant strands falling across his forehead in a sexy fashion. He had a strong jaw, full lips, and deep sea blue eyes.

"Quinn. What are you doing here?" J.M. asked.

"I went to Grace's workshop and introduced myself afterward. She knows we're friends, so she invited me for lunch."

That voice. Kara's heart thundered in her chest. Oh, God, this was her anonymous stranger.

"You must be Kara." Quinn smiled broadly, no obvious sign of recognition in his face as he offered his hand, but he absolutely knew who she was. How could he not?

She hesitated, then placed her hand in his. Immediately, a quiver raced along her arm.

"Well, buddy," Quinn continued, his gaze never wavering from her face, her hand still enveloped in his, "we're a couple of lucky guys. We're with the two most beautiful women at the conference."

He brushed his lips along the back of her hand in a delicate kiss. Her knees went weak.

Oh, God. His voice. His charm. At the same time that she wanted to crawl away and hide, she wanted to climb into his lap and kiss those devilish smiling lips of his while he wrapped his strong arms around her and pulled her close. She could imagine his cock hardening between their bodies, then it gliding into her . . . his hard, thick shaft filling her.

Good heavens. Fantasizing about hot sex in the middle of a restaurant with a total stranger . . . who'd already made love to her while she wore a blindfold last night . . . This was so unlike her. What was J.M. doing to her?

J.M. pulled out a chair and she sat down, then he sat beside her. Quinn sat facing her.

All through lunch, her blood sizzled with awareness. She barely heard their conversation, trying her best to remain invisible.

"You haven't said much, honey," Grace said over coffee. "Are you feeling okay? You seem a little flushed."

"Fine. Just a little . . . tired." Her cheeks flushed hotter as she wondered if either of the men took that as a reference to her not getting much sleep because she'd been busy doing other things in bed last night.

Quinn glanced at his watch. "Well, I hate to break up the party, but I've got to get back early to prepare for my workshop."

"I'm the only one here not giving a workshop at this conference." Although Kara wrote a sex column, she felt out of her depth with these three very real sex experts.

"You're working here in a different way." Grace turned to Quinn. "Kara interviewed Jeremy for a sex column she writes for *Urban Woman* magazine."

"Really?" He sent her a devilish grin. "Well, maybe you'd like to interview me, too. I can tell you all about Kama

130

Sutra." He winked. "And plenty of other interesting things about sex, too. I bet your readers would be fascinated."

She nodded, unable to utter a word. She was sure her readers would be fascinated by a great many things about Quinn, especially her experience with him last night.

Quinn took a final sip of his coffee and tossed some money on the table.

"If you two don't mind, I'll go with Quinn," Grace said.

"It's okay with me," J.M. said. "Kara and I can relax over coffee, and talk."

Grace picked up her purse, then smiled at J.M. and leaned toward him.

"He's great," she whispered, nudging her head toward Quinn.

Kara watched Quinn and Grace leave the restaurant, then pass by the window on their way back to the hotel.

"Grace is hoping to go out with him, right?" she asked.

J.M. nodded.

"Do you think that'll work out?"

"Probably not." He caught her gaze. "Especially since you want to see him again."

Her blood froze in her veins and she fiddled with her napkin. "See him again?"

"Come on, Kara, I know you recognized him." He leaned forward. "Look, I'm really sorry about that. I didn't mean to put you in an awkward position." He smiled and took her hand. "You handled the situation admirably."

"You think he knows?"

He chuckled. "Of course he knows." He stroked her

cheek. "I know he was dazzled by your naked beauty, but still . . . a blindfold isn't much of a disguise."

Her cheeks flushed hotly.

"Don't worry about it. He enjoyed last night . . . and he will be totally discreet. He'll never acknowledge what happened unless you'd like him to."

A ripple of excitement flashed across her skin. She licked her lips, thinking of Quinn's hard, masculine body pressed to hers.

"Why would I want him to?"

"Because maybe you'd like him to join us for another fantasy."

She gazed into J.M.'s brown eyes, hunger burning inside her. "Like what?"

He grinned. "A really popular fantasy for women is a ménage à trois. Do you want to give it a try?"

Images of J.M. in front of her, Quinn behind, crushing her between their bodies, their hard cocks delving into her, sent her pulse racing.

She drew in a deep breath and hesitated. A threesome? How could she do something like that?

Ha. This from the woman who let a total stranger have his way with her last night.

She chewed her lower lip. When had she become such a prude? They were talking about sex between consenting adults. With two experts on sex, as a matter of fact. And writing about sex was her job.

Research didn't get any better than this! How could she possibly *not* do this?

J.M. slid his arm around her waist, sending currents of need through her. "I could arrange it for tonight."

She gazed at him, wondering if she should drag him up to one of their rooms and have her way with him right now. On the other hand, anticipation—and the promise of two hot, hard guys—would make it all the better!

"Tonight would be good."

A knock sounded at the door. Kara stiffened and tightened the knot of her black satin robe. That would be her sexy stranger from last night. Quinn.

Could she really do this?

J.M. went to the door and opened it.

"Quinn, come in." J.M. stepped back and let Quinn in.

He looked so sexy in slim-fitting blue jeans that hugged his long, lean thighs, and a casual navy shirt. His gaze immediately fell on Kara. Some of his straight, light brown hair had fallen across his forehead, and he raked it back as his gaze caressed her satin-clad form. A slow smile spread across his face, lighting his deep blue eyes.

"Kara . . ." Her name sounded like silk gliding from his lips. "It's wonderful seeing you again."

His ocean blue gaze locked on hers, holding her mesmerized as he stepped toward her. She drew in a breath as he approached, forcing herself to breathe out again.

"J.M. told me you recognized me at lunch."

She nodded. "Your voice."

"Ah . . ." His lips turned up in a devilish smile. "And I thought you sensed a magical aura about me."

He took her hand and brought it to his lips. The delicate brush of his mouth sent tingles dancing along her skin.

"I am delighted you want to see me again," he said. "Ever since last night, I haven't stopped thinking about you."

He turned her hand over and pressed his lips to her palm. Her knees nearly buckled on the spot.

"J.M., are there any ground rules this evening?" he asked, releasing neither Kara's hand nor her gaze. Even though he was talking to J.M., it felt as though she and Quinn were the only ones in the room.

"The only rule is that Kara is comfortable with whatever happens." J.M. stepped behind her and placed his hands on her shoulders. "Anything to add, Kara?"

Oh, God, she couldn't think, let alone form words, so she simply shook her head.

J.M. nuzzled her ear. "Would you like some wine?"

"Yes, please." Maybe that would help calm her. This whole situation was unsettling, yet wildly exciting.

Quinn's mouth found the inside of her wrist. Tingles skated up her arm, then quivered down her spine. He kissed along her forearm, then nuzzled the inside of her elbow. She felt dizzy and excited, her blood simmering with heat. His kisses continued up her arm to her shoulder. When he pressed his lips to her neck she grasped his shoulders for support.

She gazed at him, her lips slightly parted. Her focus dropped to his lips. He tipped up her chin and dropped his mouth to hers. At the first brush of his lips, she drew in a deep breath, then surrendered herself to the passionate on-slaught of his mouth. His lips moved on hers with a masterful confidence, then his tongue nudged forward and slipped inside. She met his tongue with enthusiasm, delving into his mouth and exploring freely.

This man was so sexy and confident . . . and knew how to make a woman feel desired.

"Your wine." J.M.'s voice startled her from her delightful surrender.

She drew back from Quinn and took the wineglass from J.M. She felt a little flushed and strangely embarrassed by kissing Quinn in front of J.M. Although last night, J.M. had watched Quinn make love to her. She had had on a blindfold, which had made it feel somewhat . . . surreal. She hadn't seen either of them . . . had been totally caught up in the fantasy painted by J.M.'s words. It had been as if only she and J.M. were present. Now it was different.

She sipped her wine . . . glanced at J.M., then Quinn . . . then sipped her wine again.

J.M. ran his hands over her shoulders and smiled.

"It's okay, sweetheart. You don't have to be embarrassed."

She stared at the stemmed glass in her hand and nodded.

He took the glass from her fingers and set it on the round table, then drew her into his arms.

"I'm not jealous. This fantasy . . . you and me . . . and another man . . . I know it's exciting to you, and that's exciting to me."

"And it's sure as hell exciting to me, too," Quinn added with a chuckle.

A small smile spread across her lips and she kissed J.M.

His arms around her, his lips moving on hers, made her feel secure. And confident. She could do this.

Their kiss turned passionate, sending wild tremors through her as the hormones she'd been trying desperately to rein in finally released. Her nipples puckered and her insides seemed to melt. She stroked her fingers along J.M.'s clean-shaven cheeks, loving the feel of his masculine jaw moving as his tongue explored her mouth thoroughly.

Their tongues danced as J.M.'s hands caressed her back. Then another hand glided across her shoulder. Quinn stroked her hair to one side and kissed the back of her neck. J.M. cupped her cheeks and Quinn shifted closer, his hard chest pressing against her back. Quinn ran his hands down the sides of her ribs, sending a frenzy of sensation dancing through her. Her nipples pulsed with need and she arched forward, crushing her breasts against J.M.'s muscular chest.

J.M. released her lips and turned her around. Quinn covered her mouth with his and swirled his tongue inside while J.M. cupped her breasts. She sucked on Quinn's tongue while J.M. squeezed and caressed her swollen mounds until she gasped, dropping her head back against J.M.'s shoulders.

"Come here, sweetheart," J.M. said as he guided her backward. He sat down on the couch and eased her in front of him so she perched on the edge between his strong thighs.

Quinn sat in the chair opposite them, just a couple of feet away. She was facing Quinn, with J.M. cradling her from behind. Starting at her shoulders, J.M.'s hands glided down her body, over the black satin of her robe. He cupped her breasts and teased her nipples. Quinn watched with great interest, his sea blue gaze locked on J.M.'s active fingers. J.M. continued down her ribs. When he encountered the sash of her robe, his fingers entangled in the narrow band of fabric and she felt it release. She watched Quinn's darkening blue eyes as J.M. drew open the fabric.

Her breathing quickened as he revealed her nearly naked form, dressed only in a skimpy lace bra, panties, garter belt, and black stockings. At Quinn's heated gaze, her nipples puckered even tighter.

"You love him seeing you, don't you?" J.M. murmured in her ear.

She nodded, seeing no point in denying it. J.M. pulled her robe down her shoulders, then twisted the fabric tight around her upper arms like a binding, thrusting forward her breasts. She sucked in air at the immensely erotic feeling of being held captive in this way.

J.M. stared down at her. "They really are quite lovely." While still holding her immobilized, he stroked his free hand over one breast, then the other. He dipped one finger under the lace cup and teased her hard nipple. She arched against him. He slipped the rest of his fingers inside her bra and cupped her breast, then caressed.

She wanted more. Oh, so much more.

He released the fabric behind her and drew the robe from her arms. Then his other hand snaked around her waist and he caressed her ribs and descended to her panties. His finger trailed along the edge of the lace, then dipped underneath. She almost gasped as it curled between her legs and dipped inside. Her thighs spread wider to give him better access.

J.M. grinned at Quinn. "She is very wet."

Quinn sipped his wine as he stared intently at the movement of J.M.'s fingers under the black lace. She melted against J.M. as one finger toyed with her nipple and the other stroked inside her. A frenzy of sensations quivered through her.

He drew his hands from her intimate parts and released the hooks of her bra, then dropped the straps from her shoulders. She slid her arms free, then rested her hands on his muscular thighs, still cradling her. Slowly, he eased the lacy cups from her breasts. Cool air washed against them, making the nipples thrust forward. With both men's hot gazes caressing her, however, heat sweltered through her.

Quinn's fingers twitched as though he couldn't wait to stroke her, but he sat calmly watching J.M. caress her swollen mounds. She sighed against him, enjoying the delicate pressure of his hands roaming over her. He cupped her and her nipples peaked into his palms. His hands slid under her breasts and he lifted them.

"Quinn, would you like a taste of these?"

"You're damn right I would."

Quinn surged forward and knelt in front of her. Her breasts rose and fell with her excited breathing. He stroked over the swell of white flesh, then dragged his fingertip over one hard nub. She whimpered. He grinned, staring at the dusty rose nipple. Then he leaned forward and licked it. She dropped her head onto J.M.'s shoulder. J.M. watched as Quinn's mouth covered her nipple and he began to suck. At the same time, Quinn found her other nipple and tweaked it. Kara moaned as molten heat flooded through her.

J.M.'s hands stroked her ribs as Quinn teased her nipples. Her eyelids fell closed and she simply enjoyed the feel of a hot mouth and warm hands stroking her. Quinn sucked on her sensitive nub again and she moaned. J.M.'s hands glided down her sides, then he slid inside her panties again. He stroked over her clit, triggering wild tingles inside her, then he dipped into her. She arched upward.

"She really is ready for us."

Quinn glanced down at J.M.'s probing hand under the fabric. "Let me feel."

J.M. slipped from inside her and cupped her breasts.

Quinn kissed down her belly, then nibbled on the edge of her panties. He tugged the lace to the side and glanced at what it had been hiding. She trembled as he gazed at her curls, then slowly dipped his fingers under the fabric and cupped her. She rose against his hand . . . then he stroked her wet slit.

"You are incredibly wet, gorgeous. I can hardly wait to taste you."

She felt weak at the thought of his full mouth covering her . . . his tongue delving into her.

Quinn drew his hand away as J.M. tucked his fingers under the lace edges of her panties and drew them down. She lifted her hips so he could slide them down her thighs. Quinn took over and slid them the rest of the way off.

J.M. leaned back, tucking his hands under her and lifting her onto his hips, which raised her pelvis. She could feel the swell of his erection under her. Quinn pressed her knees farther apart and leaned forward.

At the first touch of his hot mouth on her, she moaned . . . then when his tongue stroked over her clit, she whimpered. He licked her slit, then drove his tongue into her. Her fingers tangled in his short brown hair as pleasure seeped through her. J.M. stroked her breast, occasionally tugging or squeezing a nipple. Quinn teased her with a rapid flicking of his tongue in and out, then shifted to her clit. His tongue spiraled over it as he slid two fingers inside her. She moaned at the delightful stroking and the intense pleasure quivering from her clit. Pleasure swelled through her and she gripped his head as she rode the wave. Higher. Bucking against him.

Finally, she collapsed on J.M., her entire body a boneless mass.

A chuckle rumbled through J.M. "Time for a nap, Kara?"

"Are you kidding?"

Both men laughed and J.M. sat up, easing her forward.

Quinn stood up, retrieved his wine, and took a sip. The man had too many damn clothes on. Not that it wasn't wildly sexy lying here—on top of J.M.—totally naked . . . with both men fully clothed. Like she was their plaything. She almost wanted to get up and walk around, flaunting her nudity, while playing the willing slave ready to satisfy their every whim.

But right now, she wanted to see some male flesh.

Thirteen

"Quinn, that shirt looks a little hot."

He promptly set down his glass and, grinning at her, slowly released the top button of his shirt . . . then the next. She watched as the fabric eased open, revealing well-defined muscles across a broad chest. Her fingers itched to stroke along that satiny skin stretched taut over steel-hard muscle. He unfastened the buttons on the cuffs of his shirt, then peeled it away.

She had to touch him. She stood up and walked toward him, aware of J.M.'s gaze following her naked derriere. Quinn's gaze caressed her naked breasts. Knowing both men watched her . . . and wanted her . . . sent goose bumps dancing along her skin.

She stroked her hand along his hot, hard flesh, then dipped her finger into his wineglass and stroked a burgundy smudge across his chest. She leaned forward and licked the wine from him. She dipped again and dabbed the liquid on his beadlike nipple, then flicked her tongue over it as she continued to stroke his chest. Muscles rippled beneath her fingertips as his arm encircled her. He dragged her against his body and captured her lips. Her hard nipples drove into his chest as he crushed her to him, his tongue probing her mouth, then released her, leaving her breathless and wanting more.

She stepped back a little, stroking her hand over his sculpted abs.

"Quinn, I'm a little"—she dragged her gaze from his simmering blue eyes, down his broad chest, to his crotch, and licked her lips—"hungry."

"Really?"

He unfastened his belt, then his zipper, and his pants dropped to the floor. He pulled the elastic of his boxers forward, then down. As he bent over, she got only a quick glimpse of hard cock as he peeled the boxers off. Then he stood up.

She had only felt his cock last night. Thick. Entering her from behind.

Now she stared at it. Hard . . . thick . . . curving upward.

She wrapped her fingers around it and stroked. Hot, and as hard as steel beneath the soft kid-leather skin. She stroked up and down.

J.M. stepped behind her, his hands wrapping around her waist. As she crouched in front of Quinn, J.M.'s hands enveloped her breasts. Kara explored Quinn's cock, stroking her finger over the head, then around the ridge of the corona. Her other hand slid downward and cupped the sacs underneath. She kissed the tip of his cockhead—a brief brush of her lips—then drew his balls forward. There was no hair on them . . . or anywhere on his groin . . . something she hadn't noticed last night. She'd been a little preoccupied, but the fact that he shaved his personal places delighted her. She drew one sac forward and licked it, then nibbled it with her lips.

"Oh, yeah."

At the sound of pleasure in his voice, she leaned forward and opened her lips around his ball and drew it into her mouth. She prodded it with her tongue, then gently squeezed it in her mouth. His fingers curled through her hair, his pelvis arching against her.

"Gorgeous, that is . . ."

She opened wider and drew the other ball into her mouth.

"Ohhh, so great."

J.M. stroked her hard nipples, then crouched behind her as his hands glided down her waist and over her hips. He stroked around her stomach and drew her against him, then cupped her breasts again.

She sucked lightly on Quinn, then released his sacs and licked the base of his shaft. J.M. cupped her ass and caressed in circles, watching while she licked Quinn's cock from bottom to top. Her tongue swirled around the tip of his cockhead, then around the ridge.

She covered Quinn's cock with her mouth and sucked the head inside. The hot, smooth skin filled her mouth and she squeezed it, then dove down on him. J.M.'s hand slid between her legs and stroked her slick opening while

Opal Carew

she sucked on Quinn. She stroked his balls and tightened her mouth around his hard shaft, then she sucked him deep inside. He groaned, stroking her hair from her face. Pleasure melted through her at J.M.'s intimate stroking as she sucked and squeezed Quinn's cock and caressed his balls.

"Oh, man, doll, I'm going to burst."

She nodded and hot liquid erupted in her mouth.

His spent cock slipped from her lips as yearning built within her, fired by J.M.'s insistent stroking. J.M. drew her to her feet and sat her on the couch, then stripped off his clothes. When she saw his long, hard cock staring at her, she grabbed it and stroked, then pulled it into her mouth. She dove down three times before he drew himself free and tugged her forward to perch on the edge of the couch. J.M. knelt in front of her and she wrapped her arms around him as his cockhead nudged her opening. He drove forward, impaling her in one thrust.

"Oh, God, yes."

He filled her with hot, hard cock, then pulled back and drove forward again. Quinn sat on the chair, his hand wrapped around his already swelling cock. Knowing he sat there watching them magnified the already intense pleasure of every thrust. Her vagina clamped around J.M.'s pistoning cock as it stroked her passage. The heat inside her swelled to joyful delight as he pumped into her again and again. His finger found her clit and he flicked the nub. Immediately, she burst into orgasm, gasping as she clung to him. He thrust deeper and faster until she wailed in joyful abandon, riding a long, intense wave of ecstasy.

Finally, she slumped back on the couch. J.M. leaned in and kissed her tenderly.

"God, you two are hot together," Quinn said, his voice hoarse.

J.M. nibbled her ear. "Are you ready for the full treatment? Quinn and I?"

She sucked in a deep breath and peered at Quinn. His cock was at full attention again . . . and J.M.'s still was.

She nodded.

"Okay, kneel down, facing Quinn."

She pushed herself from the couch and faced Quinn, then knelt on the floor. J.M. sat on the couch behind her and eased her forward to her hands and knees. As Quinn watched intently, J.M. stroked along her damp slit, then glided his slick fingers over her back opening. She willed herself not to tense as one finger slid inside. He moved it around in a small circular motion. A delightful sensation spiraled through her. Soon he introduced a second finger, continuing to move in circles . . . then a third. He spiraled deeper and she sighed.

His fingers slipped away and she felt hard flesh nudge against her opening. She stiffened.

J.M. stroked her back. "Relax. I'll go slow. Let me know if you want me to stop."

She drew in a deep breath and relaxed. His cock pressed forward, a little at a time, stretching her.

"Remember, breathe and relax."

She nodded, taking deep breaths. His cockhead continued forward until it filled her. She breathed out, then drew in another breath. He stroked her slit, then over her clit. She arched back at the tingling pleasure and he pressed his cock deeper into her.

She wanted more. All of him.

Slowly, he filled her until he was all the way inside. He drew her from the floor to his lap, pushing deeper still. She moaned.

Quinn stood up and approached them, his gaze shifting from her breasts to her dripping opening. He stroked her breasts, then sucked one hard nipple into his mouth. The hot sensation of his mouth on her tight bud and J.M.'s cock filling her was overwhelming.

"Oh, God, Quinn, I want you inside me, too."

He smiled. "I'm happy to oblige." He placed his cock-head against her front opening and drove forward, impaling her at once. She gasped for air, overwhelmed by the intense sensation of two hot, hard cocks filling her at once.

Her accelerated breathing made her lightheaded as the two men held her tightly sandwiched between them. She wrapped her hands around Quinn's shoulders. He tucked his hands around her thighs and lifted her legs. She wrapped them around him. He kissed her, then drew back and thrust forward again.

"Oh, yes," she cried. The intense sensations trembling through her threatened to erupt into ecstasy at any second, but she didn't want this to be over too soon, so she tightened her legs around Quinn, holding him close.

J.M. nuzzled her neck and Quinn kissed her, his lips moving on hers tenderly. J.M. caressed her breasts and Quinn moved his pelvis in a small spiral, teasing her senses. She loosened her hold on him and he drew back and thrust forward again, driving J.M.'s cock deeper, too. Heat thrummed through her. With Quinn's next thrust, she felt a wave of joy sweep through her. He thrust and thrust again. Both cocks seemed to swell inside her, and a wave of ecstasy washed through her. Her head fell back as she wailed in release. The cocks drove into her again and again, propeling her orgasm to incredible heights. She gasped and wailed again. Quinn groaned and erupted inside her. J.M. moaned in pleasure.

The three of them clung to one another, gasping. Sated and reveling in the sensual heat of their bodies against hers, she sighed. Living out this delightful fantasy had been the most sensational experience of her life.

Kara woke up in the dark, the warmth of two male bodies surrounding her. One hand stroked her breast—she wasn't sure whose. Her nipple hardened and she arched forward. The hand cupping her belonged to the man behind her, she realized as her other nipple strained against the hard chest in front of her and that man murmured, clearly just waking up. His hand slid around her hip and he drew her against his pelvis . . . and his growing erection.

She rolled onto her back and slid her hand around his erection, then glided her other hand over the other man's hips and found his hardening cock. As they both stroked her breasts, she glided her hands up and down their shafts.

"I feel like a little something to nibble," she said,

squeezing their cocks in her hands, then tugging to give them the idea to shift into position.

They both pushed themselves up and knelt on either side of her head. Her eyes were getting used to the dark, so she closed her eyes, recapturing the anonymity of the other night. A cock brushed her cheek. She grabbed it and licked it, then drew it into her mouth. She found the other in the dark and wrapped her fingers around that one, too. She released the first from her mouth and drew the second inside. She licked the tip, then sucked. This one was thicker than the other, but she pushed the thought out of her mind, concentrating on licking hard flesh, then released it and drew the other in. Hard flesh. One, then the other. She kept them moving in, then out, losing track of that brief glimpse of whose was whose.

She drew this one deep several times, then sucked hard. She released and nibbled the other cockhead with her lips, then swallowed deep. When she released it, she grasped each more firmly and guided them to her lips, then licked the tips of both of them. She opened her mouth and pressed the cockheads inside, straining wide to receive them both.

Her tongue swirled against one, then the other, then she squeezed them and sucked. Both men groaned. The cockheads filled her mouth . . . so erotic . . . and she licked and sucked as she stroked their hard shafts. She cupped their balls and kneaded lightly, then released their cockheads and guided the men forward until their balls hung over her. She brought one man's ball to her mouth and licked, then did the same with the other man's. She sucked on him, gently drawing his soft sac into her mouth, then the other. She squeezed them inside her mouth while gently stroking with her tongue. She released him, then drew the other man's balls into her mouth, giving them the same treatment. Finally, she released him.

"You both taste so good." She pushed the covers down and stroked her breasts, cupping them, then toying with the hard, puckered nipples.

The men dove down and sucked her nipples into their mouths. The feel of hot, wet man mouth on each nipple drove her wild.

"Oh, that's so good," she murmured as she stroked their heads, her fingers tangling in J.M.'s dark waves, while her hand glided over Quinn's shorter, light brown hair.

A hand caressed down her belly, then between her legs. His finger stroked her clit, then dove inside.

"She's wet," J.M. said.

She opened her legs.

"Mmm . . . and ready," she murmured.

"Well, that certainly sounds like an invitation."

"I want both of you." She drew in a deep breath. "One stroke each, one right after the other." She still kept her eyelids tightly closed.

"We can certainly oblige that," Quinn said.

They climbed off the bed. One grabbed her waist and rotated her ninety degrees on the bed and dragged her to the edge until her legs dangled over. Then he lifted her hips and the other man pressed pillows beneath her, raising her pelvis, then drew her thighs wide open.

One of them stepped toward her and a hard cockhead nudged her wet opening. His cock glided into her as he eased forward and filled her. Then he pulled away and stepped aside. She could feel him pressed against her thigh. The other man stepped into position and drove his cock into her. Deep. Stretching her. Then he stepped back. She could feel him against her other thigh.

The first cock entered her again. Then the second. Her heart thundered in her chest. Back and forth. One man after the other. Filling her. Stretching her. Driving her pleasure to soaring heights.

On the next stroke of hot, hard flesh driving into her, she grasped his hips.

"Oh, please. Keep going."

He kept pumping as the pleasure flooded through her. She moaned.

"That's . . . so . . . good . . . I'm going to . . . ah . . . I'm . . . coming."

An orgasm blasted through her, searing her senses. The cock slid from her depths and another hard cock slipped inside. He spiraled while his finger flicked her clit and she immediately climaxed again, moaning.

His cock slid free and she could hear their murmured voices. Someone leaned toward her and his lips brushed her ear.

"In the dark . . . with your eyes closed," Quinn said, "you don't really know if you're here with two men or . . . more."

Another cock thrust into her.

Bliss

"Is that a third man inside you now?" Quinn suggested.

From the direction of Quinn's voice, J.M. moved inside her now. But she ignored that, thinking of him as Three.

She moaned as Three's cock drove deep. Then strong arms circled her waist and he rolled over, taking her with him, his hard cock still firmly embedded inside her. Then another cock nudged her back opening. Number four.

Four's cock pressed insistently, stretching her. Slowly, his cockhead invaded her opening, filling her as Three's cock filled her vagina. Four eased forward until he fully impaled her.

They began to move and pleasure pummeled her from every direction. Her body went limp as they fucked her between them. Trapped between two hot, muscular bodies, hard cocks driving into her. She moaned as the pleasure intensified, then shot off the scale as ecstasy claimed her. She wailed, long and loud, her voice hoarse from the strain of expressing her joy so many times.

She gasped, riding their bodies . . . carried away by the pleasure.

One man groaned and at the feel of his liquid heat filling her, her orgasm crested one more time. Then the other grunted and heat filled her again. She gasped as she arched back against him.

Oh, God, they'd both come inside her.

They all slumped on the bed. The man behind her rolled sideways, and the man under her held her tight to his body. J.M. His hand stroked her back and she snuggled against him, his cock still inside her. She dozed, waking slightly as she felt herself repositioned on the bed, then she fell into a deep, satisfied sleep.

J.M. watched Kara, sitting beside him, take a spoonful of her soup. Quinn sat next to Kara and Grace sat next to Quinn.

Things weren't going quite as J.M. had hoped with Kara. He'd thought by now he'd have had a chance to show her more of the advantages of Tantra. The problem was, once he'd brought Quinn into their fantasy role-playing, he'd become a more important player in their relationship than J.M. had planned. After the first fantasy—with Quinn as the anonymous stranger—J.M. had planned to follow up with some Tantra fire-breathing exercises, then a slow, lingering session of lovemaking, but Kara had been in such awe of the fantasy sex, he had wanted to let her revel in it.

Last night, with the threesome, he'd assumed Quinn would be on his way afterward, but Quinn had stayed and they'd made love into the night. Not that J.M. hadn't enjoyed it, but he wasn't getting enough one-on-one time with Kara, and he needed that to make her see the two of them were meant for each other. He'd already lost out to another guy in the past, and now that he'd found the woman he knew he was meant to be with, he'd be damned if he'd let it happen again.

"The Sex-a-la-Gala event starts this afternoon," Grace commented. "It's next door in the convention center. I really wish I could skip this afternoon's sessions to attend, but I'm giving another talk. I hear they're having some great specials for those who attend early." She took a sip of her water, the ice tinkling against the glass as she tipped it.

"That sounds like a great idea," Kara said. "I could probably find some interesting ideas for my column, and I'd probably have a better chance of interviewing some of the exhibitors since it probably won't be too busy yet." She glanced at J.M., her sapphire blue eyes questioning. "Do you want to go?"

"Unfortunately, I can't," J.M. said. "I'm giving another talk, too."

Her lips compressed in disappointment.

"I can go with you, Kara," Quinn volunteered.

Fourteen

J.M. stamped down the jealousy rising in him. He and Kara were meant to be together. Things would work out as they should. Quinn was not a danger to J.M.'s relationship with Kara. J.M. was just letting his baggage get the best of him. He took a deep, cleansing breath and let his jealousy evaporate into the ether.

"That would be great," Kara said with a bright smile.

J.M. watched Kara's blue eyes twinkle as she gazed at Quinn and they talked about the types of exhibitors they heard would be there. J.M.'s gut clenched.

Kara and I are meant to be together. Things will work out as they should.

Kara showed her conference badge to the man at the door of the Sex-a-la-Gala show. Attendees of the Sensational Sex Conference were allowed in free. He handed her a brochure and waved her and Quinn through. The show had opened only an hour ago and some booths were still adjusting their displays. The hall was huge, with rows upon rows of vendors and exhibits.

"Instead of following the crowd, let's go down the far aisle and work our way back," Quinn suggested.

"Good idea," Kara said.

The number of people entering the show hardly represented a crowd, but Kara agreed with separating from the flow of people.

The sheer number of ways and materials in which the male organ had been rendered amazed Kara as they walked along the left aisle. Silicone, glass, quartz crystal, and even chocolate. Dildos, vibrators, sculptures, and candy treats. A huge seven-foot inflatable version stood along one wall, where a group of people took each other's pictures standing beside it. Several versions of the female equivalent also sat among the sea of sex toys, art, and candy treats.

"There will be some shows and demonstrations on the center stage." Quinn's gaze scanned over the brochure.

"Anything interesting?" She leaned in close and suddenly became aware of the closeness of his body and the heat emanating from him. She'd never been with Quinn without J.M., and for some reason she felt a little guilty at her body's reaction to Quinn . . . as if she were cheating on J.M.

"There'll be a burlesque dancer in a couple of minutes, a demo of a sex swing about twenty minutes after that. . . ."

Her gaze scanned down the schedule on the glossy paper. "Oh, and a demo of a bondage bed. That should be interesting. But it's not until eight this evening. We'll be at the party."

Quinn smiled. "You know it's a masquerade party."

"They said costumes are optional."

He raised his eyebrows. "So you'd rather go naked?"

She smacked him lightly with her brochure. "That's not what they meant."

"You sure? It *is* a sex conference."

She smacked him again. "I didn't bring a costume."

Quinn gestured around them. "Look where we are. I'm sure we can find something suitable here."

She pursed her lips. She loved wearing costumes. "I'm not going in some skimpy French maid costume, if that's what you're suggesting."

"Oh, I think we can be more creative than that."

Music blared over the loudspeaker, then a woman's voice welcomed them to the Sex-a-la-Gala show. Kara couldn't quite catch what she was saying, but it had something to do with the schedule.

Quinn leaned in to her side. "She's announcing the burlesque dance. Do you want to go see?"

Kara nodded and followed him down aisles past colorful booths toward the center of the large hall. The crowd thickened and she could see a raised stage ahead. Quinn took her hand and led her past groups of people so they could get closer to the stage, where she could see. Jazzy music began and a woman appeared on the stage in a blur of pastel blue feathers, sequins, and velvet. She carried a huge feather fan, which she swirled around. As she danced, she would occasionally hide behind her fan and toss aside a bit or two of her costume, then reveal herself with more bare skin on display. Finally, she was down to a glittering velvet strapless bra and panties. She wiggled her derriere and blew the audience a kiss over her shoulder, then waved her fan as she disappeared behind the curtain. A young woman in a black leather bodysuit picked up the items the dancer had discarded as the emcee thanked the dancer and introduced the next performer.

Quinn tapped her arm and pointed to the side. Kara nodded, knowing he wouldn't hear this close to the loud-speaker. She followed him several yards from the crowd.

"Maybe we should see if we can get you one of those fans," he suggested.

"As part of my costume?"

"Actually, I was thinking more if you were going nude, it would give you some cover."

She batted him again, but she had drooled over the fan. She had always wanted a big feather fan like that. She had no idea why. She just loved feathers and they seemed so . . . elegant yet provocative.

"Actually, honey, there is a booth over there that sells those fans," said a dark-haired woman with a half smile sitting at a booth with studded leather boots and sexy black corsets. "I think it's the same aisle as the erotic chocolates, which you might have seen when you came in."

"Oh, thank you." Kara glanced at the leather items in her booth, thinking she should look around after the woman was so helpful, but this was not the type of thing she'd buy.

"Let's go take a look," Quinn suggested and led her away again.

They dodged past people in the aisle, found the erotic chocolate booth, then turned down that aisle.

"There it is." Quinn stopped in front of a table with glittering rhinestones, sequins, and velvet. On the wall of the booth behind the table were several stunning feather fans in lively colors.

"Oh, they're beautiful!" Kara's eyes widened at the long, willowy, ostrich-feather fans.

"What do you think? Do you want to get one?" Quinn asked.

Her gaze caught on the price tag of one that was teal and white.

"Oh, my goodness, it's almost five hundred dollars."

A woman behind the table smiled. "That's because that one's two colors and a triple layer of feathers. If you want a single color and two layers it will only be about four hundred." She pointed to a pure white one beside the one Kara had been eyeing. "And a single color with only one layer of feathers"—she pointed to a fuchsia one that didn't look as full as the others—"is just over two hundred. All of them open to about fifty inches across and thirty inches high."

Two hundred. She bit her lip. As tempting as the beautiful fans were, that was more than she could justify for such a decadent item. Especially one she'd never actually use.

"We have kits, too, so you could assemble one yourself. You save anywhere from fifty to a hundred dollars, depending on which fan you choose."

That meant that the two-layer one—because she would

not settle for the almost straggly-looking single-layer—
would still be more than three hundred dollars. And she
couldn't imagine how it would look after she tried to put it
together. Probably like a mangy sheepdog during shedding
season.

"Thank you for your help," she said, and grabbed
Quinn's arm and tugged him away.

"I take it the fans are out. I guess we better find a costume, then." He followed her around the corner into the
next aisle, then grabbed her hand. "Over there."

She paused at a table covered with dazzling rhinestone
jewelry, but she barely got a look before he tugged her on.

"We'll come back, I promise. I just want you to look at
this." He led her to a booth a couple down from the jewelry. More leather.

She glanced at a black velvet mannequin sporting a
leather . . . uh . . . whatever it was, it was made of leather
straps and chains that didn't even attempt to cover the parts
of a woman's body she'd want covered.

"What do you think?"

She crossed her arms. "About what exactly?"

"What's more appropriate to wear to a masquerade
with a sex theme than black leather?"

"I'd be arrested if I showed up in public in that."

He glanced at the mannequin and laughed. "I wasn't
thinking of that," he leaned in close to her ear, "but I would
love to see you in it."

She trembled at his closeness, then her gaze caught on a
male mannequin wearing a silver studded leather thong.

She could just imagine J.M. wearing that, with his superb muscular butt totally on display.

He pointed at a mannequin a little farther down wearing a sexy leather bustier, a short black skirt, and spike-heeled boots.

"That's what I had in mind."

"Okay, sure, but I don't have the budget for that any more than I did for the fan." And if she did, she'd rather have the fan.

"Budget concerns, eh?"

He scanned the table and picked up a black leather collar with pointed studs.

"You could wear this."

She stared at it dubiously. "And what else?"

"Whatever you want. Black would be good. Low-cut would be exceptional." He winked. "But not necessary."

"And I'm going as what? A dog?"

"No." His eyes glimmered in the sunlight.

At the devilish glint in his eye, a quiver danced down her spine.

He leaned in and his lips brushed her ear.

"You'll be my slave."

J.M. noticed Grace waving at him as he glanced around the ballroom. She sat at one of the round tables near the dance floor. He smiled and nodded, noticed she had a drink in front of her already, then went to the bar to order one for himself. He sat down beside her and set his beer on the table.

"You didn't come down with Kara?" he asked.

"No, she didn't answer when I knocked on her door. I thought maybe she was already down here, but I haven't seen her. You two didn't go to dinner together?"

"No, I haven't seen her since lunch."

"Maybe she and Quinn went to dinner after the Sex-a-la-Gala show." She sipped her wine spritzer. "How is it going with you and Kara?"

"I've been helping her explore fantasies for her column for the past two nights. Quinn's been helping, too."

"Ah, no wonder I haven't been able to make any headway with the man."

He nodded and swirled the beer in his glass.

"The problem is, I'm not getting any alone time with her. If I did, I'd spend some time showing her more about Tantra and energy work. I don't think she'll recognize what we have until she can look beyond the physical."

"Do you have another fantasy planned for tonight?"

"No. I haven't had a chance to talk to her."

"Well, maybe I can distract Quinn so the two of you . . ." Her words trailed off as she gazed over his shoulder.

He turned around. Kara walked toward them looking stunning in a black leather bustier that pushed her breasts upward in a scintillating swell of flesh, with slim-fitting black pants, black high heels, black leather studded wristbands, and a matching collar around her neck . . . with a leash attached. Behind her walked Quinn, wearing black pants and a black leather vest, holding the other end of the leash, smiling.

"Actually, it looks like those two have devised their own fantasy for tonight," Grace said.

As soon as Kara saw Grace and J.M., she headed toward them. The leash tugged at her collar as she walked a little too fast in front of Quinn, so she slowed down again, yet still the collar pulled at her neck. She slowed down even more and realized Quinn was shortening the leash. A quiver ran down her spine at the control Quinn exerted over her movements. What would it be like to play this scenario out with more than just being on the end of a leash?

Quinn coiled the black leather strap around his hand and held it a couple of inches from the back of her neck, keeping her by his side.

"Good girl. Let's play this up."

She'd left her long, dark hair flowing loose over her shoulders. Quinn stroked it behind her ear, giving a better view of her swelling breasts, leaving her feeling very exposed.

His gaze lingered. "I'm glad you decided to buy the bustier after all. It's very becoming."

Second thoughts about wearing the daring garment quickly faded with his heated stare and the simmering heat of J.M.'s gaze as he watched her approach. Wearing this, she felt wicked and sexy.

As she glanced around the ballroom, she noticed that only about a third of the people wore costumes. Not all that many, but enough so she didn't feel totally ridiculous. Of course, it helped that Quinn had donned black jeans and a studded leather vest. They were obviously a pair.

When they arrived at the table, Quinn released the

coils of leather from his hand, but the leather loop remained around his wrist.

"Well, that's a different look for you, Kara," Grace said.

Kara sat down beside Grace, and Quinn settled beside Kara, across from J.M.

J.M.'s gaze glided over the leash to her tight-fitting bustier, then lingered on her breasts as they swelled above the leather. Her breath caught in her throat at his stark male scrutiny. "So why aren't you two in costume?" Quinn chided.

"I guess we're just not as fun-loving as you," J.M. said.

"So, Quinn, you have a slave. What kind of commands do you intend to give her?" Grace asked.

"I don't know." He winked at Kara. "We'll see as the night unfolds."

Her stomach fluttered as she wondered what type of mischief he might have in mind. He reached for her collar and released the leash, then handed her two drink tickets.

"I'd like an imported beer," he said. "Get something for yourself." He glanced at Grace. "Would you like something, Grace? Or J.M.?"

"Sure, I'll have the same as Quinn," J.M. told Kara.

Grace laughed. "All right. Make mine another wine spritzer."

J.M. and Grace each handed her a ticket. Kara stood up, realizing she'd probably be the waitress for the rest of the evening. And providing whatever other *service* Quinn would require. As she stood in line at the bar, the man behind her kept glancing at her cleavage. She had to stop herself from

Opal Carew

crossing her arms over her chest. She ordered the four drinks, making hers a screwdriver, then realized she couldn't carry them all.

"Here, you can use this," the bartender said as he grabbed a round tray from the table behind the bar and set the four glasses on it.

She took the tray, balanced it on one hand, and steadied it with the other as she walked across the crowded ballroom, trying to avoid being bumped and spilling the drinks. When she arrived at the table, she set down the tray and passed each person a drink, feeling every bit the serving wench.

"Good girl," Quinn said as she sat down.

She almost expected him to give her a treat to nibble.

Then he leaned in and kissed her. As his lips pressed against hers, she did nibble a little, then dove her tongue into his mouth. Good heavens, could the idea of being his slave be turning her on?

He nuzzled her ear. "You know, I think J.M. is feeling a little lonely," he said. "Why don't you go over and give him a kiss, too? In fact, I think you should sit on his lap."

She stood up and walked around the table to J.M., settled her hand on his shoulder, then sat on his lap. She felt wicked and . . . controlled. She stroked her hand across his cheek, then kissed his lips. She continued to stroke his face as she nibbled his lips, then flicked the tip of her tongue into his mouth. His arms wrapped around her and he pulled her close, then his tongue dove between her lips as he consumed her mouth.

After a long, fervent kiss, he drew back.

"So, you're Quinn's slave." He hooked his finger in the loop at the front of her collar and tugged, pulling her face closer to his. "Do you obey only his commands?"

A slow smile spread across her face as she gazed into his simmering chocolate eyes.

"I . . . think with two such commanding men, I might find myself serving two masters."

He tugged harder on the loop, drawing her closer, then he captured her lips. The feel of his firm, masterful tongue invading her mouth sent shivers through her body.

He kissed her ear and murmured, "I can hardly wait to get you back to the room."

Her gaze locked with his and she wanted to go right now.

"Kara, time to dance." Quinn stood beside her, his hand extended.

She smiled at J.M., then took Quinn's hand and stood up. Quinn attached the leash to the ring on her collar, then led her to the dance floor. He coiled the strap around his wrist as he drew her into his embrace.

After two dances, J.M. cut in. Quinn handed him the leash and J.M. drew her close, then his strong arms slid around her and he guided her to the music. A few moments later, Quinn and Grace danced past them. Grace smiled brightly at Quinn and Kara felt a little guilty that she'd been monopolizing Quinn for the past few days when Grace clearly would like a go at him.

"You've been enjoying your fantasies?" J.M. asked.

"They've been very exciting." She smiled. "You and

Quinn are extremely . . . talented." She gazed into his eyes. "It's quite something how you two are so willing to . . . share."

J.M.'s mouth twitched a little. "As long as you're enjoying it, that's the main thing. So you and Quinn decided on a little dominance and submission fantasy for tonight?"

"Well, it was just an idea we got for the costume while we went around the Sex-a-la-Gala show today, but . . . if you like the idea . . ."

He drew her close and nuzzled her ear. "I think it's an extremely sexy idea."

The song ended and the band announced that they'd be taking a break. J.M. escorted her back to the table, where Grace sat waiting for them. J.M. sat down between Kara and Grace.

"Quinn's gone to get another round," Grace said.

Kara glanced toward the bar and saw Quinn in a long line, chatting to a trio of very attractive men who were also in costume, though more elaborate than Quinn and Kara's. One wore a gladiator costume and the other two wore black leather with bare chests, crisscrossed with leather straps and chains, revealed from under their black leather vests. They glanced her way and Quinn smiled. The others gazed at her with melting hunger in their eyes.

Fifteen

Kara watched as Quinn and the three strangers progressed through the line, then her eyes widened as the strangers strolled back to the table with Quinn.

"J.M., Grace, *Kara* . . . this is Lou, Trent, and Jeff."

Lou wore the gladiator costume that consisted of a white tunic overlaid with brown leather armor, which covered his chest with leather strips hanging from below a wide leather belt to cover his groin area. Leather gauntlets drew attention to the bulging muscles of his arms and legs.

Trent and Jeff wore black leather. Both men had incredibly well-defined chests and arms. Trent had leather suspenders with chains linked across his chest. Leather straps strained across Jeff's chest.

"Hi," Grace said, eyeing Lou with a smile.

"Do you mind if the fellows join us?" Quinn asked.

Kara glanced at J.M., who shrugged. "Sure," she said.

Trent sat beside Kara, with Jeff beside him. Three of the eight chairs from their table had been borrowed and

Opal Carew

taken to other tables, so Quinn and Lou retrieved a couple from a nearby table where the occupants had left. Quinn set his beside Grace, and Lou sat down between Quinn and Jeff.

"Trent and Jeff are both doctors and Lou is a hypnotherapist."

"Really?" Grace said, smiling at Lou. "J.M. does hypnotherapy, too, and he's told me a lot about it. There seem to be a lot of fascinating applications. I find it quite intriguing."

Lou nodded. "There are." He leaned forward and began chatting to Grace.

The music started up again and Kara couldn't hear most of what Lou and Grace said. Quinn stood up and gestured for Lou to switch seats, since clearly Grace and Lou had a lot to talk about.

"How about you?" Trent asked Kara. "What do you do?"

He gazed at her with striking brown eyes, and she shifted in her chair.

"I . . . write a column for a magazine."

Quinn crouched beside her. "A sex column." He smiled as she glanced at him, her cheeks heating. "What? You do." He took her hand. "Let's dance." He turned to Trent and Jeff. "Excuse us."

Quinn led her to the dance floor. "Sorry if I embarrassed you. I didn't think you were embarrassed about your job."

"I'm not really, I just . . . I guess I'm never quite sure how a man is going to react and I'm . . . careful."

"You're worried he'll make a pass at you?"

168

"That type of thing."

"Trent and Jeff won't make a pass at you . . . but they would like to have sex with you. Lou, too, but it looks like he might be distracted by Grace and, unless you actually want five men rather than just four, I think we should let them distract each other."

Her eyes widened. "Five men?"

His eyebrows arched up. "So you do want all five?"

"No . . . I mean . . . I just want to know what you're talking about."

"Okay, so I was talking to the guys in line and—I didn't just meet them, by the way. I've sat with them in a few of the conference sessions over the past few days and we've chatted. They're all really nice guys. Very respectable, too."

"But they want to have an orgy with me?"

"I'm not sure it's an orgy with just one woman and five men."

"What is it then?"

He grinned. "A woman's dream come true?"

She paused.

"Well, isn't it? Five men who find you so attractive they're willing to share you just to be with you. And they all want to satisfy your every whim."

Her heart fluttered and she glanced at Trent and Jeff. All muscles and good-looking masculinity.

"On the other hand, if we keep with our theme of the night, you might be satisfying *their* every whim, which ultimately means them giving you intense pleasure."

She shook her head. "This is a crazy conversation."

"What if I were to order you, as your master, mind you, to go and kiss each of the men passionately?"

She trembled but shook her head.

"Ah, that would be too public, wouldn't it? I could order you to slide under the table and unzip those leather pants of theirs, then . . ."

Her mouth went dry and she shook her head. "I couldn't do that."

He leaned in to her ear. "Last night you experienced a ménage à trois, and I take it you enjoyed it. You didn't know me at all, other than having had anonymous sex with me the day before, while blindfolded. You had never even seen me before."

Her cheeks burned at his words.

"You trusted J.M. to bring me into your fantasy," he continued. "Why not trust me to introduce you to an incredible experience with four men? You'd be making their fantasy come true, too. You see, Trent and Jeff are a couple, but they've wanted to try being with a woman. You have definitely struck their fancy. Think of it, you are so alluring, you've actually turned the heads of two men who usually aren't attracted to women."

She pursed her lips. "So they're really bi, right?"

He grinned. "Maybe a little bit. But they have been exclusive to each other since they started a relationship, and Jeff has never actually been with a woman. Trent has wanted to have the experience of sharing a woman with Jeff for a long time. Now it seems they're both intrigued by you, and we all thought experiencing a joint fantasy would be pretty sensational. Since they're a couple, there'll be no complications later. And they totally respect you, just as they hope you'll respect them."

Somehow he made the whole thing sound like a reasonable proposition . . . but . . . living out a fantasy with four men? At the same time?

She glanced at Trent and Jeff again. Trent's charismatic smile, paired with Jeff's slightly shy one, charmed her completely.

Oh, God, she could feel her barriers crumbling.

"I don't know that J.M. will like the idea."

"Are you kidding? If you like the idea, I'm sure he'll love the idea." He loosened his arms around her and stepped back. "Let's go ask him."

He led her back to the table and she sat down next to Quinn as she watched him lean toward J.M. and whisper in his ear. J.M.'s gaze locked on her. She couldn't read anything from those dark chocolate depths, but she felt her breath stop as she waited for the decision.

He gave one nod.

Her stomach fluttered as if filled with butterflies. She glanced across the table at Grace, who gazed entranced into Lou's eyes. Quinn murmured something to her and she nodded, barely tugging her gaze from Lou's.

A moment later, she felt pressure from the collar as Quinn gave a playful tug on the leash. She stood up and followed him. J.M. walked beside her, his hand on the small of her back, and Trent and Jeff followed behind them. The elevator felt crowded when they stepped aboard, even though they were the only people on it. The four men standing around her were all so big, both in height and build. Muscles and testosterone filled the small space.

As Kara walked into the room, the men following her—*four* of them!—she trembled inside. Could she really strip down and have sex with these two strangers . . . and at the same time with J.M. and Quinn?

The fantasies with J.M. and Quinn so far had opened a whole new world for her. Both men had been essentially strangers when she'd had sex with them. She'd had several hours to get to know J.M. first. Quinn was a total unknown their first time. She hadn't even been able to see him . . . yet the whole situation had been titillating and had sent her to wildly ecstatic heights.

Even just the thought of being pinned against the pole, then Quinn's hard cock gliding in and out of her, sent her hormones rocketing. Now she'd have the opportunity to have four men give her pleasure . . . adore her body . . . take her to climax.

Quinn tugged on the leash and led her through the sitting room into J.M.'s bedroom, where the pole still stood prominently in the open space. He unlatched the leash from her collar, then pulled a carabiner clip, similar to the one she used to attach her water bottle to her backpack when she went cycling, from his pocket and walked behind her. He drew her hands behind her back and she felt the cold metal of the pole against her arms, then felt him tug on the rings on her wrist straps and heard a click. She tugged on her wrists to confirm he'd clipped them together . . . behind her back and around the pole, thrusting her breasts forward.

Quinn dragged his finger along her arm as he stepped around her again.

He grinned at her and stared at the swell of white flesh bursting from her bustier.

"You're a vision, gorgeous. Now, you're going to be a good little slave and obey everyone's commands, right?"

J.M. and the other two men—Trent and Jeff—all stared at her with hunger in their eyes. A quiver ran through her. Here she stood, her hands bound behind her back . . . helpless to their whims. Her insides melted with heat.

Jeff ran his hand through his wavy, short brown hair, his blue eyes bright with anticipation. Trent glanced from Jeff to Kara and smiled, a glint in his intense brown eyes. With his dark hair brushed back from his face and hanging to just below his ears, he looked a little like Johnny Depp, the effect enhanced by his self-assured, confident stance.

Quinn's fingers stretched wide as his gaze trailed down her body. "Now . . . where to start."

"Quinn, why don't we let Trent and Jeff do some . . . exploration. Then we can just follow their lead," J.M. suggested.

Quinn grinned. "Excellent idea."

J.M. sat down at the small table by the fireplace and Quinn joined him, still smiling broadly.

Trent and Jeff exchanged glances, then Trent nodded and stepped toward her. She trembled. Would he strip off her clothes first? Or tug her breasts free so they tumbled from their leather prison?

Instead, he tugged the leather vest from his shoulders . . . and Jeff followed suit. Then Trent stepped closer still, his broad, nearly naked chest brushing her arm. Hard, muscular flesh. His finger stroked along her cheek and he leaned in and kissed her, teasing her lips with delicate little nips. Jeff stepped to her other side and when Trent released her mouth, Jeff leaned in and captured her lips. He tucked his finger under her chin and tipped up her face. Then his tongue stroked the seam of her mouth and eased inside. She opened and welcomed him with her tongue.

He drew back and smiled. "Sweet."

She didn't know if he meant the sensations or her taste. Trent and Jeff locked gazes, then they kissed each other, their faces close in front of her, their mouths moving passionately. They parted and smiled at her. Trent drew her face to him and kissed her again, this time delving between her lips with his tongue. As he explored her mouth, Jeff stroked her hips, then she felt the button on her pants release, then heard the jagged sound of the zipper unfastening. Slowly, as Trent continued to consume her mouth, Jeff drew her pants down her legs to her ankles. He knelt down and unfastened the straps on her shoes. The delicate brush of his fingertips against her ankles sent tremors through her. He removed one shoe, then the other. . . . As Trent kissed across her jaw and down her neck, Jeff drew away the garment around her ankles and stood up, then began kissing the other side of her neck. All she wore now was her leather bustier, which ended at her waist, and a black thong. Besides the collar and cuffs. Jeff stepped back and stroked down her thigh to her calf, then back up.

"Lovely legs." His hand continued over her hip and along the side of her ribs to her shoulder. Goose bumps rippled over her skin. "I can't wait to touch these beautiful breasts." His fingers grazed the swell of skin bulging from the bustier.

As Trent continued to nuzzle her neck, she felt his hand rest on the small of her back, then glide to her bare behind. He cupped her and stroked. "Firm yet smooth and soft."

Jeff smiled and cupped her other side. As they both stroked, white lightning flashed across her skin. Hot and electric.

"Everything is so perfect." Jeff kissed her again, then held her gaze with his blue eyes. The gentle adoration there sent warmth rippling through her. "I want to see your breasts."

She nodded. Both men began unfastening the hooks at the back of her bustier, one from the top and the other from the bottom. As they peeled the leather from her body, both men stared at her with utter admiration. Her nipples peaked, wanting to be touched. Jeff reached for her in awe and stroked the underside of her breast, then lightly over the nipple with his fingertips. Trent cupped her. Her nipple pressed firmly into his palm. Trent nuzzled her neck . . . tingles quivered through her . . . then he kissed the swell of her breast. Suddenly, his mouth shifted and she sucked in air as his hot mouth covered her straining nipple. Jeff covered her other nipple and they both sucked.

She dropped her head against the pole and moaned.

"It sounds like the guys are pleasing our little slave girl."

Kara's gaze shot to Quinn, then J.M. She'd actually forgotten the two men looking on. Quinn's hard cock towered from his pants as he stroked it. J.M. simply watched with a simmering gaze as Trent and Jeff sucked her breasts. Jeff leaned back and lifted her breast in his hand, then his thumb brushed her nipple. Trent continued to suck. Jeff stroked down her ribs, then along the top of her thong. Trent released her breast and slid his fingers under the elastic at the back of her thong. Jeff tugged the elastic at the front and together they drew the garment down her legs and off.

Now she stood naked in front of them. Jeff knelt down and stroked over her dark curls. Exciting tingles rippled through her at his touch.

"I've never seen a pussy up close." He stroked again. "It's quite pretty."

Trent turned to J.M. and Quinn. "Why don't you come and help us?"

The two men stood up immediately. Quinn shed his pants and socks as he stepped toward them, then tugged off his leather vest and tossed it aside. He stepped behind her and cupped one of her breasts. J.M. stroked her other breast and kissed her on the mouth, his lips caressing hers, then he joined Quinn behind her. As big masculine hands stroked her breasts, Jeff continued to explore her pussy with his fingers and his gaze. Trent kissed her thighs, then pressed them apart a little. He stroked between her legs, his fingers more daring than Jeff's as they penetrated her slick opening.

"She's wet. Feel."

Trent drew his hand aside and Jeff stroked her.

"That's lovely."

"There's a folding stool by the dresser," J.M. said.

"Oh, man, you've thought of everything," Quinn said as Trent grabbed the vinyl upholstered stool.

He opened it and set it by the pole, then eased Kara around to sit on it.

"Open your legs, gorgeous," Quinn said. "Let them see you."

She leaned back against the pole and opened to them.

Jeff stroked her wet opening, then both he and Trent knelt in front of her. They both began on a different thigh and kissed . . . moving inward . . . until they both licked her slit. They stopped to kiss, then Jeff licked her and Trent found her clit with his fingertips. He dabbed it. She sucked in a breath.

"Let me try," Jeff said.

He touched her, watching her face as she moaned softly. Jeff smiled, then licked her. Her breathing accelerated and he swirled his tongue over her, then sucked lightly.

"Mmmm."

Trent stood up and shed his pants, then presented her with his long, hard cock. The head was slender and the shaft curved upward. She licked her lips in invitation. He pressed the tip to her mouth and she opened and allowed him to glide inside, then she wrapped her lips around him and squeezed. He glided forward, filling her mouth, then drew back.

Opal Carew

Jeff licked and sucked on her as Trent glided forward again. Pleasure welled through her at Jeff's attention to her clit and her eyes fell closed. She sucked hard on Jeff . . . and almost cried out as a hot mouth covered each of her nipples. Pulsing pleasure rippled through her as the mouths sucked on her nipples at the same time that Jeff sucked on her clit. Trent's cock dropped from her mouth as she moaned.

Oh, so close. She could feel the ripples start within her.

"Jeff, you're going to make her come," Trent murmured.

Someone's fingers glided inside her and stroked her wet passage. Tumultuous sensations ripped through her, igniting an intense orgasm. She gasped and arched as several hands stroked her body while mouths licked and sucked. She rode the wave of pleasure.

Once it subsided, she heard the clip unlatch from her wristbands and J.M. took her hand and led her to the bed.

"Guys, take off your clothes and sit," Quinn directed. J.M., Trent, and Jeff shed their clothes, then joined Quinn perched on the side of the bed.

Kara's gaze wafted across the four hard cocks standing at attention.

"Kara, I want you to suck Jeff's cock," Quinn said.

She knelt in front of Jeff and licked the tip of his cock, then she leaned down and lifted his clean-shaven testicles and licked them.

He stroked his fingers through her long hair, drawing it back from her face. "That's great."

She nibbled the soft flesh, then drew one ball into her mouth. He groaned as she rolled it around inside her warmth.

She released it, then licked from the base of his cock to the tip, then she swallowed his cockhead, which was much broader than Trent's, into her mouth. She sucked, then dove down on him, taking his whole shaft into her mouth.

She cupped his balls and dove down and up, sucking on him until he felt steel-hard. She released him, then shifted to Trent. She grasped his curved cock and stroked, then sucked his cockhead. She bobbed up and down a few times, then shifted to Quinn. Quinn's familiar cockhead filled her mouth and she sucked, then she released it and licked down his cock to his balls. She drew one into her mouth and sucked lightly, then licked up his shaft again. One more purposeful suck, then she shifted to J.M.

He caught her chin and kissed her. His hot chocolate gaze heated her even more than the hard cocks in her mouth had. She licked his big, round cockhead, then drew it inside. It filled her mouth. She dragged her tongue along the ridge, then swirled over the tip. He groaned. She dove downward, then sucked him deep.

"Hey, gorgeous, don't forget us," Quinn said.

Reluctantly, she released J.M., then moved back to Quinn. She bobbed up and down on him, then moved to Trent . . . then to Jeff.

"I'd love to see one of you two fuck her," Jeff said, gesturing to Quinn and J.M.

Quinn raised his hand before J.M. could respond. "Well, I guess someone has to do it." He stood up and took Kara by the hand, drew her to her feet, then into his embrace. He kissed her passionately, then scooped her up.

"How about the ottoman?" Jeff suggested. "Her on top of you."

Quinn set her down in front of the armchair by the fireplace and he pulled the large overstuffed ottoman forward and sat down.

"You heard him, slave. Hop up." Quinn lay back.

She knelt on the ottoman, her pelvis over him. She wrapped her hand around his cock and pressed it to her slick opening, then lowered herself onto him. Her insides quivered as his rock-hard cock filled her.

"Oh, yeah." Quinn wrapped his arms around her and captured her mouth as he held her tight to his body, his cock fully immersed in her.

She felt a slick, hard cock brush her backside. Staying in Quinn's embrace, her upper torso pressed tight to him, she raised her derriere, leaving her back end exposed. Trent stood beside J.M. and stroked her hip. That meant Jeff's cockhead now stroked over her back opening.

She heard a condom package tear open and the cock moved away. A moment later, his hand stroked over her behind.

His slick fingers slipped inside her . . . first two . . . then three. . . . He swirled in circles, spreading his fingers apart a little . . . then a lot. He drew them out, then pressed his cock to her again and pushed forward. His cockhead pushed into her . . . a little at a time . . . stretching her . . . until it was fully inside.

She moaned and pushed against him. He pressed forward, the rest of his long shaft gliding inside. The incredible sensation of two hard cocks filling her sent her pulse sky-rocketing.

"God, that is so incredibly sexy." Trent stood up and moved behind Jeff.

"Oh, yeah, Trent." Jeff's cock drew out a little as he pulled back.

In the dresser mirror, Kara could see Trent push into Jeff, then Jeff push deeper into her again. The thought of Trent's cock driving into Jeff and Jeff's driving into her sent a thrill through her. She glanced at J.M. standing alone beside them. She reached out and grabbed his hard cock and drew it to her mouth. She squeezed him in her mouth as Trent drove forward again, driving both Jeff's cock and Quinn's cock deeper into her. It felt as if both Trent and Jeff filled her from behind while Quinn filled her in front. And J.M. filled her mouth.

Four hot hard cocks fucking her. Trent drove forward and she groaned as the three cocks drove deep again. She swirled her tongue around J.M.'s cockhead and he moaned. Quinn drove back, pushing her against Jeff . . . and Trent. They found a rhythm with Trent and Jeff driving forward, then Quinn driving back. Her insides rippled with pleasure and heat blasted through her at each deep, surging thrust. She moaned, losing J.M.'s cock. She grabbed him in her hand as she sucked in air, then the next thrust catapulted her into orgasm. Waves of pleasure encompassed her as a surge of ecstasy propelled her to heaven.

The men groaned, one after the other, in a domino effect of orgasms. They collapsed together, gasping for air.

Finally, Trent and Jeff slipped away. Then Quinn kissed her and she stood up. Somewhere along the way she'd released J.M., which was just as well because in the sudden surge of pleasure, she might have done him damage.

She gazed at J.M., then took his hand and led him to the bed.

"I don't want you to feel left out," she murmured.

She lay down and he prowled over her, then his hard-to-bursting cock found her slick opening and drove inside. She gasped and clutched her arms around him. He drove into her again and again, stroking her insides with incredible pleasure. Before she could catch her breath, heat blossomed inside her and a powerful orgasm tore through her, searing every nerve end.

"Oh, God . . ." She clung to him as the joyous pleasure increased to an impossible intensity . . . until it erupted through her in an explosion of pure ecstasy.

He brushed her clit with his fingertip and swirled his cock. Time and space stretched to new dimensions as her body melded with the ecstatic pleasure to become pure joy.

His body pressed tight to hers, his hard cock pulsing inside her. She sucked in air as her heart rate slowly settled to normal.

"Now, that, my friends," Quinn said with a chuckle, "is how it's done."

Sixteen

When Kara awoke, she was lying in J.M.'s arms, her head resting on his chest, with Quinn tucked up behind her. She glanced around and noticed Jeff and Trent had gone. She seemed to remember each of them giving her a kiss good-bye before she tumbled into sleep.

Feeble rays of sunlight glimmered from the edges of the drawn drapes. She glanced at the clock. Six fourteen.

J.M. shifted, his arms tightening around her possessively. She could hear his heartbeat under her ear and the closeness of his hard, warm body made her feel safe and loved.

Oh, damn. A cloud of confusion wafted through her brain. She'd had an amazing life-altering time at this conference and she knew it was all thanks to J.M. She knew it was a rare man indeed who would share a woman he had feelings for with other men in order to give her the sexual experience of a lifetime.

She felt Quinn's hand caress her hip. He was a wonderful man, too, and she'd tried to distract herself from her intense feelings for J.M. by getting closer to Quinn. He was a great guy and a sensational lover. Why was it so different with J.M.?

J.M. shifted and his lips caressed her temple in a gentle kiss.

"You're awake early," he murmured.

"True, I'm feeling a little"—she dragged her hand down his chest, over his sculpted abs, then rested her fingertips barely brushing the tip of his twitching cock—"restless."

His cock swelled and she lightly brushed her fingers over the hot shaft.

A warm hand stroked over her behind.

"Did I hear you say you're feeling restless?" Quinn mumbled in a sleep-hoarsened voice. He rolled toward her and his lips played along the back of her neck, sending tingles dancing down her spine.

She curled her fingers around J.M.'s cock and rolled onto her back. She stroked along Quinn's hip and grasped his firm cock.

A cock in each hand. Hard and ready. A great way to start the day.

She stroked them both. J.M. cupped her breast and Quinn leaned in to suckle her other nipple. She arched, encouraging their lovely attention. Quinn stroked between her legs, feeling the accumulating moisture. She felt so hot, she could barely think straight.

And she wanted immediate satisfaction.

She squeezed the two erections in her hands, stroking them harder.

"Mmm. I'm so turned on," she murmured. "I want both of you inside me."

She sat up and rolled around to plant a quick kiss on J.M.'s lips, then crouched over him, facing his feet. She grabbed his erection and pressed it to her slick opening, then lowered herself onto it.

God, he felt so good inside her.

She lifted herself up, then placed J.M.'s cockhead to her ass and slowly lowered herself onto his slick cock. His cockhead stretched her, then filled her opening.

"Oh, yes." She kept lowering herself until he was fully embedded inside her.

She lay back and J.M. cupped her breasts and drew her against his body. Her head rested on his shoulder and he nuzzled her ear. Quinn knelt in front of her, his knees between hers but around J.M.'s. He pressed his cockhead to her vagina, then slid inside.

She gasped at the exquisite sensation.

Quinn positioned himself over her, propping himself up with his arms, and drew his cock out, then pulsed forward again.

"Yes, that is so . . ." She moaned as pleasure pulsed through her as both cocks pushed into her. She squeezed her internal muscles, increasing the intense sensations.

Quinn pumped into her, thrusting faster and deeper, driving J.M. deeper into her, too.

She clung to Quinn's shoulders. He kissed her as J.M.

nuzzled her neck. Her pulse accelerated and joy erupted through her. She gasped as her entire being exploded in orgasm.

And it went on . . . and on. . . .

Like riding a wave of pure pleasure. Her body . . . and her soul . . . seemed on fire.

She peaked and seemed to expand to another realm.

Slowly . . . so slowly . . . she settled back to the real world. Sensed the two bodies sandwiching hers. Hard cocks still embedded inside her.

Oh . . . my . . . God.

She'd never experienced anything quite so intense.

Could this be the whole-body orgasm J.M. had told her about?

But how? Could it have something to do with J.M.'s Tantra expertise?

Although she didn't like the idea of elevating sex to something beyond pure physical pleasure, there seemed to be something to Tantra. J.M. had talked about energy. And not just with sex. He had helped her with her fear of flying . . . or rather of takeoffs. She couldn't deny the fact she'd felt something when he'd touched her—an intense warmth that had calmed her body and mind. And, to be honest, just being around J.M. made her feel open to ideas and points of view she'd never considered before. He made her want to expand her boundaries and open herself to new experiences that would allow her to explore new sides of herself.

Maybe she'd have to reconsider her ideas about Tantra and what it was all about.

Kara needed a break from the conference and talks about improving one's sex life. They only led to chaotic thoughts about J.M. and how he had already improved her sex life a thousandfold. Could the great sex between them have anything to do with Tantra, or was it just that he was an exceptional lover?

And how could she go back to regular sex with other men?

She decided she'd go to the Sex-a-la-Gala show to find inspiration. The sexual fantasies J.M. and Quinn had been helping her with had been extremely exciting. Maybe she should explore those more so that she could understand what excited her and bring that into her sex life when she returned home.

She wandered along the aisles, gazing at all the brightly colored sex toys, leather outfits, strappy high-heeled shoes, and naughty lingerie. She stopped at one booth with rhinestone strands hanging from a display stand. She touched one glittering strand, then let it glide between her fingers.

"You attach those to your bra to replace the bra straps," an attractive young clerk said to her. She pointed to the glittering rhinestone strap at her own shoulder and tugged the top of her black camisole down enough that Kara could see how it attached to her black bra beneath. "You just take off the strap and replace it with these. Instant glamour!"

"Very pretty," Kara said.

"With these you can wear a regular bra under a strapless top and they become part of the outfit. A pair is only twenty-five dollars. You can't beat that."

Kara liked glitz, so she purchased a pair and continued down the row with the small black plastic bag in her hand. At the end of the aisle, she gazed at a mannequin wearing thigh-high black boots with spike heels, a leather bustier with matching leather gauntlets, and a whip in her hand.

The very sexy outfit stirred Kara's interest, but the whip wasn't her thing. She didn't see herself as a dominatrix. Several leather collars hung along the back wall of the booth, some adorned with pointy studs, some with rounded studs, some with chains. She remembered the collar and leash she'd worn to the masquerade, then how Quinn had pretended to be her master. Tingles danced along her spine at the excitement of being commanded to be a sex slave to four men. She could totally enjoy being touched by them . . . being given pleasure . . . giving them pleasure. Their cocks in her hands . . . in her mouth . . . then plundering her body.

Oh, God, she liked being dominated and . . . controlled. Maybe even more than she'd experienced so far.

Many of the collars had matching wrist cuffs, which had rings on them.

A young man working in the booth noticed her interest and snapped a carabiner clip onto one cuff.

"You can attach the two cuffs together to act like

handcuffs," he said. "Or you can clip them to a chain, or to a device, like a punishment bench."

She smiled and nodded, not even wanting to know what a punishment bench was.

"Some have soft padding on the inside and can be used for suspension." He picked up a pair and showed her the inside, where she could see puffy, soft-looking lining.

"Suspension?"

He smiled. "Right. Let me show you." He attached the carabiner clip to each of the padded cuffs, then clipped them to a heavy leather strap draped over a large hook attached high on the booth wall. He then pulled the other end of the strap, pulling the cuffs upward.

"Of course, a leather strap wouldn't be a good idea for suspension. You'd want to have a heavy chain, plus a heavy-duty hook attached to the ceiling."

She tried to ignore the shimmering heat washing through her at the thought of J.M. attaching her wrists to a chain above her head, then pulling it upward until she hung from her wrists, her feet dangling below her. Then J.M. would have his wild way with her. Tearing the clothes from her body. Touching her everywhere. Then forcing her to submit to him. She would struggle and scream . . . enjoying every minute of it.

"For more ideas, you can check out the dungeon. We're doing a demo over there in about an hour."

She nodded, feeling like a bobblehead doll. "Thank you."

She turned away and walked along the aisle, knowing exactly what fantasy she'd like to act out next.

J.M. sipped his beer as he watched Kara finish her last bite of lasagna, then put down her knife and fork. He'd love just to sweep her away from here and take her back to his room and spend the afternoon making love. They'd had a lot of time with other people and precious little time alone. Even now, not only were they lunching with Grace and Quinn, but Jeff, Trent, and Lou had joined them. If he was ever going to convince her that he was the right man for her, he needed more time with just the two of them. He knew he couldn't convince her to spend the whole afternoon together, since she had conference sessions she wanted to attend, but maybe he could find a way to spirit her away for a little while.

Kara placed her cloth napkin on the table and finished the last sip of her white wine, then turned to J.M.

"I was thinking of heading back a bit early." She smiled. "What about you?"

J.M. grinned. It seemed the lady wanted some time alone, too.

Grace turned from her conversation with Jeff. "I'm almost finished, Kara. Want me to join you?"

"No, it's okay, Grace. I want to talk to J.M. about research for my article." She patted Grace on the shoulder. "You stay and enjoy your conversation with the guys."

His heart clenched. It was great that she wanted to keep this just the two of them, but the thought that it was just to pick his brain about Tantra for her article didn't make him feel particularly wanted. At least, not for the right reasons.

He drew out her chair, then retrieved her coat from the hook along the wall and held the garment out for her. Once he had his own coat on, they opened the door to the blustery weather outside. The walk back to the hotel took only a few minutes, then they stepped into the warm lobby.

"I need to put my coat away and collect my conference bag. Want to come up to my room for a bit?" she asked.

"Of course."

They rode the elevator to her floor, then walked to her room. Once inside, he took her coat and hung it in the closet, then hung up his. When he turned to face her again, she slid her hands around his shoulders and kissed him. Her soft, full lips on his sent his hormones into a spiral. He slipped his tongue into her mouth and swirled, tasting a hint of white wine.

Her hands stroked over his chest, then to his waist. She walked backward, tugging him along by the belt.

"We have a little time before the afternoon sessions start. I know you like to be slow and thorough, but do you think you can manage a quickie?"

Seventeen

J.M.'s fingers found the button on the back of her skirt and released it, then slid the zipper down.

"Try me."

He pushed her skirt over her hips, then let it fall to the floor. She tugged open his belt and freed the zipper. His pants fell with a clunk. He nuzzled her neck, loving the feel of her soft skin against his lips. Loving the soft murmur of approval in her throat even more.

He backed her toward the bed, but she shook her head.

"That way," she suggested, pointing to the wall beside the dresser.

He grinned and nodded. He backed her against the wall and stroked over her hips, then under her blouse. With her back pressed firmly against the wall, he cupped her breasts, delighted to feel her hardened nipples press into his palms through the lace of her bra. He stroked around behind her and unfastened it. In a quick movement, he grasped the hem of her blouse and pulled it over her head, ignoring the buttons down the front entirely. Her bra straps dropped from her shoulders and the bra clung tenuously to her gorgeous full breasts. He drew the garment away, then gazed at the dusky rose nipples so beautifully puckered.

"Lovely," he said as he ran his fingertips over one hard bead. He leaned forward and licked it, then sucked it into his mouth.

He felt her hand stroke over his erection, then glide into his navy briefs. When her soft hand encircled him, he thought he'd lose it right there.

God, he wanted her. Quick would definitely not be a problem.

Her breast pulled free of his mouth as she slid downward. She knelt in front of him and gazed lovingly at his hard cock. She kissed the tip.

"Oh, yeah, sweetheart," he murmured.

She smiled, then opened her mouth to swallow his cock head inside. The incredible warmth made his groin ache with need. Her tongue swirled around him, then she dove downward, swallowing most of his shaft. She bobbed up and down, and it felt as if he was making love to her mouth. His cock throbbed with need.

He grabbed her shoulders and drew her upward again, then captured her sweet lips with his. Her tongue invaded his mouth with enthusiasm.

She pushed her underwear to the floor, then kicked it aside.

"Push me against the wall," she murmured. "*Take* me."

Ah, so she wanted to be dominated. He grabbed her

wrists and pressed them over her head, then pressed his body tight to hers, crushing her to the wall. He clutched her wrists in one of his hands while his other slid down her body, squeezing first one breast, then the other. He continued to her belly, then glided between her legs, finding the moistness there. He grabbed his cock and pressed it to her opening.

"I'm going to *take* you now."

He captured her lips and thrust his tongue into her in quick, insistent jabs. She moaned into his mouth.

He drove forward, thrusting his cock into her in one long, hard stroke. Watching the look of pure rapture on her sweet face, he drew back and plunged into her again.

"You are helpless to me." He drove into her again.

She moaned, her eyelids dropping closed. With her cheeks flushed crimson and her long, dark eyelashes fanning across her cheeks, she looked like a wanton angel.

He thrust into her again, loving the feel of her hot body surrounding his aching cock. He was so close. He could hold it . . . he prided himself on holding back his ejaculations . . . but he wanted to fill her with his seed. It felt almost primal. A need to conquer his mate and make her his . . . body and soul.

"I'm . . . oh . . . going to . . ."

He thrust deeper. Faster.

"Yes . . ." She arched against him, then began to moan.

"Open your eyes. Look at me," he insisted.

He wanted to see her. Her eyelids opened and she gazed at him, her sapphire eyes dark with desire.

"Oh—" Her wrists jerked forward against his hands and her whole body stiffened.

He thrust again and again, watching the ecstasy blossom on her angelic features. At her soft gasps, then long, rapturous moan, he felt his own climax erupt into her, followed by an earth-shattering orgasm. He moaned in absolute bliss.

She dropped forward against him and rested her head against his shoulder. He released her wrists and she wrapped her arms around his waist.

Right now, he felt incredibly close to her. In fact, he felt like the most important person in the world to her. And it was a wonderful feeling.

She nuzzled his neck, then drew back and gazed at him. "Thank you. That was great."

He grinned. "Anytime."

She laughed, a soft, wispy, intensely feminine sound that stole his breath away. If she decided to walk away from him, it would leave him totally empty inside.

He couldn't let that happen. He had to convince her how much he loved her . . . and how much she loved him. Because she did love him. He could feel it. If only she would allow herself to connect with those feelings.

He captured her lips and kissed her deeply . . . passionately . . . showing all the love welling up in him.

Kara slipped from J.M.'s hold, breathless, and glanced around at her scattered clothing.

Oh God oh God oh God! The way he'd kissed her . . . the

intensity of it . . . She was afraid that any minute now he'd tell her he loved her.

She gathered up her clothing and scurried into the bathroom. She closed the door and leaned back against it, trying to catch her breath . . . to calm her erratic heartbeat with long, deep breaths.

She was allowing him to get too close. She was allowing *herself* to get too close.

Okay, she'd come to a lot of important realizations about herself since she'd met J.M. She understood that she avoided intense relationships for fear they'd tear her heart to shreds. She couldn't stand the thought of giving her whole heart away to someone who would leave her, but plunging headlong into the most intense relationship of her life wasn't the answer. It was all happening too fast. She needed to take a little time to center herself, maybe find a good therapist to help her sort things out.

If she just put a little distance between them . . .

A knock sounded on the door.

"Kara, is everything all right?"

Her heart thundered in her chest. "Um . . . yeah. Just a second."

She tugged on her clothes, then pulled open the door.

J.M.'s warm hand covered hers. "I can tell you're overthinking things." He leaned forward and kissed her temple. "Just surrender to the moment and enjoy the present. Let me help."

Kara took a deep, steadying breath. J.M. was right. She had no idea whether or not they'd have a future together.

But suddenly that didn't matter anymore—all that mattered was the here and now.

J.M. grabbed a couple of juice bottles from the fridge and sat down at the table. About ten minutes later, Kara returned, fully clothed, and sat across from him. She poured some juice into a glass and took a sip, then gazed at him.

"I've been thinking about the sexual fantasies we've been acting out and I thought up another one I'd like to try."

"Really?" He smiled. "And what would that be?"

"I . . . thought it would be fun if . . ." She blushed, then took a sip of her juice. "Well, if you were to . . . kidnap me. You know, hold me captive and . . . maybe chain me up."

"Take you against your will?"

Her cheeks flushed hotter as she gazed down at her juice, then nodded.

"I think that would be . . . very exciting." In fact, his cock already stood at attention.

She smiled and shifted around the table toward him, then wrapped her arms around his neck and kissed him. He drew her into his lap and deepened the kiss, reveling in their closeness.

When their lips parted, she smiled at him. "Thank you for helping me with all these fantasies. I really appreciate it."

"You don't have to thank me. You know I'm enjoying it, too."

She nodded. "Well, I really have to be getting back to the conference."

She stood up and grabbed her conference bag from the dresser.

"So, will you ask Quinn about it?"

J.M.'s heart sank. "Quinn?"

"About the kidnapping fantasy. I was hoping you two could surprise me with where and how you snatch me away."

His emotions raw, he wanted to ask why she wanted Quinn there, why he wasn't enough for her, but the shining excitement in her eyes at the prospect of the two of them kidnapping her for a night of forced seduction sent his cock throbbing, which dulled his brain far too much for cognizant thought.

Kara jerked from sleep as a hand wrapped over her mouth. Adrenaline shot through her, sending her heartbeat thundering.

"There's no point in struggling. You cannot escape."

J.M.'s voice. Her fear turned to excitement. *Her fantasy!*

"Do you understand?"

She nodded.

"Now I'm going to have to gag you so you don't scream."

He pressed a ball into her mouth. A strap wrapped around her face and he fastened it at the back of her head.

The feel of the rubber ball pushed into her mouth was very sexy. He fidgeted behind her and suddenly a cloth slipped over her eyes. She felt his fingers play over her hair as he tied the cloth at the back of her head.

He stood up and hoisted her over his shoulder, her body draped over him and one of his arms draped carelessly over the backs of her thighs. He carried her across the room.

Was he carrying her into the hall? Surely someone would see them. But within moments, he laid her on a bed.

Someone took hold of her ankles. *Quinn!*

A strap encircled her ankle, then she heard a click. She tugged her ankle, but it wouldn't move. He pulled her other ankle to the left, pulling her legs wide apart, then wrapped a strap around it. She heard a click, then he released her. She tried to pull her legs together, but the straps prevented her.

"Don't bother struggling."

She started at the feel of Quinn's breath on her ear.

"You are our prisoner," J.M. said.

A hand caressed her breast and her nipple instantly pebbled.

Someone leaned toward her ear.

"Your safe word is 'cat,'" J.M. murmured in her ear. "If you can't speak, for any number of reasons"—he tapped the ball in her mouth—"then snap your fingers or slap your hand on something three times. Like this." He took her left hand and thumped it on the bed, then he moved away.

One man grabbed the hem of her nightshirt and tugged it over her head. She sucked in air at the sudden feel of cool air on her naked body.

"Well, isn't that convenient. No panties."

A second later, each man took one of her wrists and

199

pulled it upward, away from her body. Straps encircled them, followed by clicks. Now she lay totally naked and spread-eagle on the bed. She couldn't see them, but she could feel their hot gazes.

Someone leaned in to her ear again.

"We're going to have our way with you. Both of us," Quinn said.

He caressed her breast, then rubbed his thumb over the tight bead. J.M. covered her other nipple with his mouth and sucked on it, then dragged his teeth over the sensitized nub. She trembled at the intense sensation.

Someone reached behind her head and the gag released, then slipped away. She felt something warm against her face, then brushing her lips.

"Open," Quinn commanded.

She opened her mouth and his cockhead pushed inside. J.M. continued to suck on her nipple while he caressed her other breast. Quinn pushed his cock deeper into her mouth, then drew back, then pushed in again. J.M.'s hand crept down her stomach, then slid between her legs, stroking her moist slit. Two fingers impaled her. Oh, God, his touch was driving her wild.

"She's very wet."

Quinn thrust into her mouth. J.M. thrust his fingers in and out of her slit. She arched toward his hand as she sucked on Quinn.

"Fuck her, man," Quinn said.

Oh, it was moving so fast. She arched forward, wanting J.M. to take her. Wanting it fast and hard. She felt his cockhead press against her . . . then he impaled her with one sudden thrust. She moaned. Quinn's cock fell free.

"You like that, don't you, doll," Quinn said.

He held her jaw and pushed into her mouth again. J.M. thrust into her, then pulled back, his cockhead dragging along her vagina, sending tremors of need through her. Quinn thrust into her mouth in short strokes. J.M. thrust forward, then ground his hips against her, his cock buried deep inside her. She tightened her intimate muscles around his thick cock.

"I'm going to come in your mouth, gorgeous." Quinn thrust again, then she felt him tense. Another thrust, then hot liquid erupted in her mouth.

Quinn pulled free and J.M. began to thrust. Long, hard strokes. Driving deep inside her. She arched against him as powerful sensations plummeted through her. His hard, thick cock pulsed and she squeezed him, desperate for the promise of release rising in her.

"Oh, please. Make me come," she begged.

He drove harder. Faster. Quinn licked her nipple, then sucked mercilessly. She wailed, then arched, and her muscles contracted. Ripples pulsed through her and she seemed to tremble everywhere. A roaring thunder of pleasure ripped through her, exploding in a fierce orgasm.

J.M. pulled free and she gasped for air. Then another cock pressed against her and thrust deep. Quinn. He thrust, then swirled. She moaned. He started a rapid rhythm of thrusts . . . then stroked her clit with his finger. She plummeted into orgasm again, wailing her release.

He drew away, then she felt her wrist pull free with a click, then the other. Then her ankles were freed. A strong pair of hands flipped her over . . . on her hands and knees on top of a hard male body. His cock glided into her and he pulled her against his muscular chest. The other man lifted her buttocks, then his cock pressed against her back opening and pressed forward . . . stretching her . . . filling her.

"Now we're both inside you. Fucking you," Quinn said from behind her, his hand coiling in her hair and drawing her head back gently. "And you like it, don't you?" He nibbled her neck.

"Yes." At their simultaneous thrusts, she wailed. "Oh, God, yes."

Her breasts crushed against J.M.'s muscular chest and both cocks drove deep inside her. Hot, hard male flesh invading her body. Filling her with astonishing pleasure.

"Tell us that you like us fucking you."

They drove deep again.

"I . . . like you . . . fucking me."

"You want us to fuck you deep and hard," Quinn prompted.

"I . . . want you . . ." she moaned, "to fuck me. . . ."

They quickened their pace.

"Oh, yes . . . deep . . . and hard."

J.M.'s cock glided along her slick inner passage. An astounding wave of joy swelled inside her, then pleasure pummeled every cell of her being.

"Oh . . . please . . . *harder.*"

They thrust harder. Filling her impossibly deep.

She stiffened, consumed by mind-blowing pleasure.

"You're coming, aren't you?" Quinn asked.

She nodded, unable to utter a sound. She felt suspended in time, pleasure washing over her . . . wave after wave.

"Tell me, gorgeous," he murmured against her ear.

"I . . ." She gasped, then sucked in air. "I'm . . . coming."

The men pounded into her harder and she wailed as the orgasm blasted up a notch. She clung to J.M. and rode the pleasure.

Quinn jerked and she felt his cock pulse inside her. He relaxed and drew free from her body. Just as she felt her body relax, J.M. stroked his hand along her back, sending tremendous heat thrumming through her, then he pulsed forward several times. She gasped as another orgasm blossomed through her, then J.M. exploded inside her. Flames consumed her as white-hot pleasure rippled through her. She soared to heaven, her entire body rippling in ecstasy. Then she lost consciousness.

Eighteen

"Sweetheart? Kara? Are you okay?"

Kara opened her eyes to see J.M. leaning over her.

"All right?" All she could remember was mind-numbing pleasure. She reached for him and drew him toward her. "Oh, yeah."

She captured his lips and he kissed her, his lips moving on hers with passion.

Quinn stretched out on the bed behind her.

"So our little captive likes being used by two forceful strangers."

She raised her hands over her head and pressed her wrists together, thrusting her naked breasts forward.

"Yes, I'm a very bad girl. I should be punished."

J.M. grabbed her wrists and pressed them tight to the bed. His cock brushed her slick opening, then glided inside. He thrust a couple of times.

"Punished, eh?"

He pulled free and she realized that was punishment in

itself. He rolled to sit on the side of the bed, then pulled her onto his lap, facing away from him. Quinn hopped off the bed and moved in front of her as J.M. drew her legs apart, lifting her knees in the air. Quinn knelt in front of her and drew her legs toward him, then positioned her feet on his shoulders. J.M. leaned back, pulling her with him, until they were both almost lying down, then Quinn pushed his cock inside her. It went incredibly deep. She moaned.

He thrust a few times as J.M. stroked her tight nipples, then rolled the tips between his fingers. Quinn thrust again. Oh, so deep. Intense pleasure rocketed through her. Exploding within her. A staggering orgasm pulsed through her. Quinn kept thrusting as she rode the wave of pleasure.

Quinn cupped her face and kissed her, his tongue gliding into her mouth briefly, then he released her.

"You know, some of the more difficult Kama Sutra positions could be easier with three. Like J.M. holding your legs there and keeping you slightly propped up."

"That was a Kama Sutra position?" she asked.

"Yes, the filling of the well." He grinned. "Although the woman isn't usually lying on top of another man."

"I think we should get back to her punishment," J.M. suggested.

Quinn smiled and strode to the adjoining door, which Kara realized was open. That's how they'd gotten her here. They'd taken her to the room that adjoined hers.

Quinn returned a moment later with her collar and leash, then fastened the collar around her neck. He connected the leash, then tugged. She followed him.

He sat down on one of the chairs at the table and J.M. sat on the other.

"Suck my cock," Quinn demanded.

She crouched in front of him and took his flaccid cock in her hand, then wrapped her lips around it. It immediately swelled in her mouth, soon filling it. As she sucked, she felt J.M. wrap his hands around her hips and lift, until she was on her knees leaning forward into Quinn's crotch. J.M. stroked her slit, dipping his fingers in a little occasionally. She sucked Quinn and bobbed up and down on him. J.M. knelt on the floor and licked her slit. She moaned around Quinn's shaft. J.M. dabbed at her clit, then suckled lightly.

"I'd like some of that," Quinn said. "Captive, turn around and suck his cock."

She released Quinn and turned around, immediately missing J.M.'s mouth on her. She wrapped her fingers around J.M.'s already swollen cock and licked the tip, then dove down on him. Quinn's mouth covered her clit and he teased it with his tongue. She sucked hard on J.M. After several intensely pleasurable moments of Quinn's attention, he slipped away. She released J.M.'s cock from her mouth and licked him from base to tip like a giant lollipop.

Quinn glided his legs between her knees and under her, then tugged her body downward. His cock brushed her wet slit and then slid into her . . . backward from what she was used to. He grasped her hips and thrust her up and down, driving his cock deep inside. She grabbed J.M.'s cock like a handle and stroked it hard and fast, mirroring Quinn's thrusts inside her.

Quinn groaned and erupted inside her. She gasped in orgasm. Immediately, J.M. lifted her onto his lap and impaled her. Still quivering with her first orgasm, she clung to J.M. as he thrust into her. He stroked her insides with his hard cock, his hands gliding along her back as if drawing energy up her body. Intense pleasure rocketed through her and she moaned in complete surrender. Her consciousness fragmented and she collapsed against him in trembling ecstasy.

As she rested against him, sucking in air, waiting for her heart to find a normal rhythm again, she wondered how she could continue to endure such complete and utter rapture.

And, once she went home, how she'd ever learn to live without it.

Kara watched the waitress fill her cup with steaming coffee, then Grace's. Kara added a teaspoon of sugar, then poured in a little cream, the confusing thoughts that had kept her tossing and turning all night still wafting through her brain.

"What do you think about Tantra?" Kara asked.

Grace stirred her coffee, tapped the spoon on the side of the cup and set it down, then gazed at Kara.

"Is it Tantra you want to know more about, or J.M.?"

Kara sipped her coffee. "Let's start with Tantra."

"I believe in it, if that's what you're asking. It's a very powerful discipline. It helps people find a higher level of awareness."

"I thought it was sexual energy."

"Yes, and sexual energy, which is the creative energy that fuels our soul, helps us open up to the universe. To connect with others and embrace love."

Kara arched her eyebrows. "So Tantra energy is for people in love?"

"Kara, there are many kinds of love. I'm not saying that Tantra is only for those who are soul mates and plan to live happily ever after. Every sexual relationship can benefit from Tantra. Even solo, you can benefit from Tantra."

Before she'd come to this conference, she would have rolled her eyes at that. But after everything she'd seen and felt since meeting J.M., she was surprised at how open she felt to the idea.

"J.M. told me there's such a thing as a full-body orgasm. He said it's an energy thing someone does on their own."

Grace smiled. "I've read about them, but I haven't tried one myself. If J.M. knows how to help you have one—which I bet he does—take him up on it. It would be an incredible experience."

After lunch, Kara decided to take a short walk outside in the crisp, sunny afternoon. Snow crunched under her feet as she walked through the park down the street from the hotel. She sat down on a bench and gazed across the frozen pond.

As she enjoyed the brisk air and the peaceful setting, she began wondering if there was more to love than she'd thought. She'd always thought love was nothing more than a chemical reaction in the brain. Sure, romantics glorified it with their talk of soul mates and finding the One, but they were just deluding themselves. Weren't they?

She shivered despite the sun shining brightly in the clear blue sky. It was too cold just to sit, so she stood up and walked along the pathway through the frozen park.

Concern for J.M.'s feelings plagued her. If things didn't work out, it would be incredibly hard for her, but she would survive. But J.M. didn't seem to have the tough shell she'd developed over the years. What if *she* ended up breaking *his* heart? Could she live with herself if she destroyed his optimistic view of love?

Which was becoming more and more difficult because she had begun to realize the universe was not as simple as she'd thought. When J.M. made love to her, she felt something far greater than she felt with Quinn—or any other man. Maybe there was something beyond the physical.

Was it love? She didn't know. She leaned against a black wrought-iron fence overlooking what was probably a garden in the summertime. Could there actually be something beyond the physical? Could there be something more than just sex? An energy aspect? Or what J.M. had called Chi in his workshop?

But how could she know for sure? Maybe she should keep exploring with J.M. If she'd come this far in just a few days, she knew there was still more in store for her.

J.M. needed to find Kara. She had run off to her room first thing this morning to shower and change before he'd been able to set up a time to meet with her for lunch. He still desperately wanted some time alone with her. He'd been encouraged when she'd taken him to her room yesterday for a quick bout of lovemaking. He'd felt close to her and almost sensed she'd started to realize she returned his feelings of love . . . then she'd suggested Quinn join them for the kidnapping fantasy. Now he wondered if he'd only been imagining her feelings for him, seeing what he wanted to see.

He knew if they were meant to be, things would work out. He kept reminding himself of that and took comfort in the belief. It's how he'd lived his life for a long time.

Yet . . . now he wondered. . . . Could he have been wrong about Kara? Wrong that she was the manifestation of his dreams . . . his desire for the perfect woman. He knew that sometimes the little barriers that got in the way of his goals were sent to test his determination to move forward in his life in search of his true happiness. But sometimes they were actually signs that he had turned down the wrong path. Could it be that he wanted to find the woman of his dreams so much, that he'd been hurting from having to move on from his past relationship so much, that he'd simply convinced himself to believe that Kara was the perfect woman trotting into his life right on cue?

His heart thumped in his chest at the thought of giving her up. No, he loved her. He could feel it in every fiber of his being. Now he desperately needed the time to convince her to return his love.

He'd sneaked out of the last workshop of the day before it ended in hopes he could head Kara off before she ran into

Grace or Quinn. He really wanted to ask her to join him in his room for some intimate time alone.

People began streaming past him . . . more and more until the hallway was filled. He glanced across the crowd, watching for her. After about ten minutes, the stream of people thinned. He didn't know for sure if she'd passed him in the midst of a horde of people, but he waited.

Then he saw her as she stepped from one of the meeting rooms.

Damn, Grace walked along beside her. Now he wouldn't get a chance to steal Kara away. The two women glanced his way, then Kara smiled. She leaned toward Grace and murmured something, then Grace smiled and nodded. The two approached him.

"Hello, J.M." Grace said, smiling broadly.

"Hi," Kara said, with almost a shy expression.

"Well, I'll see you two later," Grace said, then strolled away and disappeared into the retreating stream of people.

Before he had a chance to react, Kara laid her hand on his arm. Heat shimmered through him at her delicate touch.

"J.M., I was wondering if . . ." She smiled. "Um . . . could we go to your room . . . or mine. I . . . have something to ask you."

He smiled, his heart thumping in his chest at the thought of having her all to himself.

"Of course." He offered his arm and she linked her hand around his elbow.

Moments later, they stepped from the elevator and strolled down the hallway toward his room. Once inside, he closed the door and immediately turned to her and drew her into his arms. The brush of her lips under his sent his groin tightening and his heart pounding. He wanted her so badly. Even more, he wanted to convince her she loved him . . . just as much as he loved her.

She melted against him. He felt her need wash through his body, melding with his own.

Then it ebbed. Just a little, but the feel of it slipping away sent panic skittering through him.

She pressed her hand to his chest and drew back from the kiss.

He gazed down at her sweet face.

"J.M., I asked you here for a reason. I . . . need to learn a little more about Tantra. For my article."

His heart froze. Here he held her in his arms, full of passion and desire, wanting to join with her in an intimate bond of love . . . and all she wanted to do was pick his brain? To use his expertise?

Damn it, had he really been wrong about her being his perfect woman? His soul mate?

He drew back, reining in his frustration and resentment, and walked across the room. He opened the bar fridge and pulled out two bottles of cranberry juice. He grabbed two glasses and set the lot on the table, then sat down.

"Fine. What do you want to know?"

For a few moments, Kara had almost forgotten why she'd suggested coming here. The heat of his hard body against hers . . . the potency of his masculine aura . . . drew on her passions like the tides to the moon. She wanted him to take her. Push inside her and drive her to ecstasy.

But she had to resist those urges. She had to find out . . . to understand *why* he had such a potent effect on her.

She sat down across from him and opened the nearest bottle, then poured the red juice into one of the glasses.

She glanced at him as he poured his juice, then took a sip. She sensed tension emanating from him. Leaning back in his chair, his long legs crossed, he seemed relaxed, and nothing showed in his expression, but . . . he didn't smile. It occurred to her that he always seemed to be smiling at her. Sometimes it wasn't obvious—just a light in his eyes—but now she felt an uncomfortable distance between them.

She felt a shiver rush across her skin. She missed the usual warmth of his smile.

"I . . . uh . . . When we spoke about Tantra during our interview, you told me about something called . . . an energy orgasm."

He nodded.

"You said you could walk me through one if I was interested."

A small grin crept across his face and it felt like the sun had come out from behind a cloud.

"And you'd like me to do that now?"

She simply nodded, too affected by his smile to utter a sound.

He glanced at his watch. "Do you need to be anywhere at a particular time because"—he gazed deeply into her eyes, setting her hormones into a spiraling dance—"this might take some time."

Her eyes widened at the promise in his voice. His eyebrows arched up.

"No, I . . . don't have anywhere else I need to be."

His smile broadened. "Good. Then take off your clothes."

Nineteen

A shiver ran through Kara.

"I thought you didn't need to touch me."

"I don't, but you lying on the bed naked will . . . inspire me. You want me to be at my creative best, don't you?"

"Um . . . of course."

She stood up and removed her blazer, then hung it over the back of the chair. As she began to unfasten the buttons of her blouse, she became increasingly aware of J.M.'s gaze following her hands. As her blouse parted and her wispy lace bra became visible, she found herself feeling . . . shy. This made no sense. She'd been naked in front of him many times. They'd not only made love, he'd watched her making love to another man . . . actually several men.

But as the blouse glided from her shoulders and landed in a heap on the floor, followed by her skirt, she realized this was different. She unfastened first one stocking, and rolled it off her leg, then the other, then stood up and discarded the garter belt. She stood there in a skimpy bra and thong while he sat fully clothed, watching her.

Her nipples puckered, pressing against the sheer black lace. His gaze stroked over them and a spike of need jolted through her. Her vagina clenched at the sharp yearning.

She turned her back to him, needing to break the intensity between them, if only for a moment. She sucked in a deep breath. What was wrong with her?

He stood up and stepped toward her, then his fingers played along the back of her bra. Goose bumps danced along her skin at the delicate touch of his fingertips . . . then the bra released. She grasped it to her body with one arm, then slipped the straps from her shoulders, her back still toward him . . . which she suddenly realized left her backside naked to his view.

Good heavens, get ahold of yourself.

She slid the bra from her body and dropped it on the floor. She drew in a deep breath, then turned to face him again. He smiled as he openly gazed at her naked breasts, causing her nipples to pucker even more. She smiled, then quickly tucked her thumbs under the elastic of her thong and pushed it down and off, before she lost her nerve. She stepped out of the flimsy garment, then stood up.

The intensity of his gaze as it wandered her body sent heat to her cheeks.

He chuckled. "You're not actually turning shy, are you?"

"Of course not." She turned and walked toward the bed. "Now what?"

"Just stretch out and get comfortable."

Comfortable? Not freakin' likely.

But she sat on the bed and lay down, then folded her hands on her stomach, feeling very odd indeed. Like being naked on a psychiatrist's couch.

"Bend your knees."

She drew her feet toward her body, which pushed her knees upward.

"Okay, now draw in a deep breath," he said.

She took a long breath in, filling her lungs, then slowly released it. He asked her to breathe deeply several more times, and she found her tension slipping away.

"Close your eyes and relax. Forget about me sitting here. I'm just a voice guiding you. Release any thoughts you may have. Completely empty your mind. Let your tensions seep away. Just listen to the sound of my voice."

She pushed away the thoughts crowding through her head and allowed her limbs to go limp.

"Take a deep breath. Inhale through your nose and exhale through your mouth. Inhale . . . then exhale. Think of the air traveling downward into your body, then circling upward as you exhale. Now the next breath . . . in . . . and out . . . Think of the air flowing in a constant circle through your body.

"Good. Now arch your lower back on the inhale, then flatten on the exhale. This will rock your pelvis up and down. At the same time, squeeze the muscles at the opening of your vagina when you exhale."

She followed his instructions, drawing the air in a circle through her body, rocking her pelvis up and down . . . and squeezing. Within moments, she felt an erotic flood of sensations.

"Squeezing like this stimulates the clitoris and G-spot while pumping energy through your entire body."

Her clit felt . . . happy. She felt . . . needy.

"You might want to allow your knees to open and close like butterfly wings. Do what feels natural to you."

She found her knees opening as she inhaled, closing as she exhaled.

"Allow yourself to be aware of the erotic feel of the contractions . . . of the sensual energy filling you with every breath."

Heat built within her, filling her insides with yearning.

"Remember when I held my hand between your legs to show you how to direct energy into your base chakra?"

She nodded, remembering the intense sensations.

"Good. Now think of energy flowing from the earth into your body through your base chakra . . . flowing up to your sacral chakra, just below your navel . . . then circling back down . . . forming a circle of flowing energy. Heat is building . . . hotter and stronger."

She felt the energy flowing through her lower body . . . heat building . . . a blaze of sensations . . . yearnings . . . needs.

"Now think of the energy moving higher . . . to your solar plexus . . . forming a circle between that and the sacral chakra."

She felt external heat over her ribs and her eyelids flipped open. J.M. stood beside the bed, the flat of his palm hovering over her, just below her breasts. It felt like his fingertips lightly touched her skin, but his hand was a good six inches above her.

He smiled. "I just want to help you move the energy."

She nodded and closed her eyes again, then concentrated on the energy flowing as he'd directed. Her knees continued to open and close with her breathing. The heat above her solar plexus intensified. She assumed that was because of J.M., but when she opened her eyes again, his hand was no longer over her.

"You're doing fine. Now allow the energy to move higher . . . to the heart chakra . . . then circle back down through the solar plexus."

She felt a rush of emotions flood through her and she felt as if she were going to cry. She stared at him, blinking back the unexplained tears.

His gaze turned somber. "It's okay, Kara. This is a healing process, too. You're probably hitting a block. Just keep breathing and allow old pain to be carried away with your breath, then released when you exhale. Breathe and release. Let go of the pain."

She didn't know what pain he meant, but the burst of emotions subsided, allowing her to feel the building sensations inside her. Excitement quivered through her.

"Now bring the energy up from your heart chakra to your throat chakra. Making sound will help the energy move higher."

She made a small sound and he chuckled.

"Kara, just let go. Open your throat and let the sound flow."

He positioned one hand over her chest and the other over her throat. Incredible heat whooshed through the two chakras and she moaned.

"Very good."

Her eyelids fell closed and she moaned again. The arching of her pelvis increased. Intense waves of heat washed through her. It felt very much like . . . when she was close to an orgasm.

"Now to your third eye." His lower hand moved above her forehead as though stepping up a ladder. "You're doing very well, Kara."

Although she was engrossed in the flood of heat filling her body, a small part of her wondered at the sight she must make, with her pelvis rocking up and down, her eyes closed, moans emanating from her throat. But J.M. was the most nonjudgmental person she'd ever met, so she let herself relax and continue.

"Now circle the energy from the throat to the third eye."

She didn't have to see it to know his hand had shifted over her forehead. As the energy moved higher, the yearning inside her increased. The waves intensified. She moaned louder.

"Now from the third eye to the crown." His hand brushed the top of her head.

The fire burning inside her intensified. Flames blazed

through her. White-hot pleasure filled her vagina and raged upward through her body, then burst out the top of her head. She moaned at the exquisite sensations. Every cell filled with complete bliss as she cried out, her fists clenched at her sides, her pelvis rocking.

"Beautiful, Kara. Keep riding the wave."

At his words, the pleasure increased, carrying her higher and higher. Time became meaningless as the pleasure of her body expanded to fill her entire consciousness. Infinite. Forever. A heavenly state of ecstasy.

She felt transformed. Drawn into another plane of being. Suspended in a perfect and harmonious moment of bliss.

"Kara?"

Kara opened her eyes, a little disoriented. She'd lost track of time . . . even where she was. Now she felt the bed beneath her. Became conscious of J.M. standing over her. She felt totally . . . fulfilled.

Yet she wanted to feel J.M.'s touch. To join with him. To share this perfect state of being.

She opened her arms and he smiled. His clothes dropped from his body with a few quick movements, then he lowered himself onto her. His cock pressed against her vagina and she wrapped her legs around him, opening to him.

His hard cock pushed inside her, gliding deep. She moaned at the feel of him inside her. He captured her lips and kissed her deeply as he drew back and glided deep inside her again. She cupped his ass and pulled him tight into the cradle of her thighs. He thrust into her again and again and she moaned in pleasure. The energy flared again and she gasped, then wailed on his deep thrust. Pleasure burst from every cell as she clung to his shoulders.

"Yes, J.M. Yes!"

He groaned as he thrust into her again and again. As her orgasm blossomed to a higher level, she felt an intense connection with him, as though they'd become one being, filling the universe with their divine pleasure.

Finally, a sense of time and space returned and she lay snuggled in J.M.'s arms, aware only of the wonderful sense of peace surrounding them.

He rolled sideways, pulling her into a warm embrace. He nuzzled her ear, then stroked her hair.

"I love you, Kara."

The moment he said the words, J.M. felt her tense up. Good God, how could the woman deny her feelings for him after that? Every time he made love to her, their connection became stronger. He knew she felt it. He was sure she loved him. Why did she keep denying it?

He propped his elbow under his head and stared down at her.

"Kara, maybe we should talk about this."

She sighed deeply, then nodded. She stood up and retrieved her clothes, then pulled them on. He followed suit, not happy with the distance this put between them.

She sat in the easy chair and he sat on the edge of the bed.

"J.M., at the beginning of the week, you asked me to

keep seeing you and explore the possibilities of a relationship between us."

She gazed at him and what he saw in her sapphire eyes tugged at his heart.

"This week has been an emotional roller coaster for me. Things are moving way too fast. I feel totally off balance. I mean"—she gazed at him, her blue eyes imploring—"we've only known each other for a few *days*."

J.M. leaned forward. "Don't you see? That doesn't matter. When you find your soul mate, it doesn't take years to figure out that you belong together. You know right away."

"But I didn't even believe in soul mates a week ago. And now I'm not sure what I believe about anything."

"Kara—"

She shook her head. "You're so sure about us, but . . . I'm not. You want me to tell you I love you, but"—her hands rolled into fists—"I just can't do that."

J.M. stood up and walked toward her, then crouched in front of her. He rested his hands on her shoulders. "Kara, I think it's just your fear holding you back. If you just allow yourself to—"

Kara stood up, pressing past him. "I'm sorry, J.M. I can't lie to you and tell you I feel something I don't."

She paced back and forth, clearly anxious to escape. His gut clenched as he realized he was losing her.

She gazed at him, her eyes shimmering. "I think I'd better go now. I . . . ." She hesitated, then stammered, "Thank you for everything."

His heart thundered in his chest as she walked toward the door, opened it, then silently walked out.

Kara stepped off the elevator, an image of the hurt in J.M.'s warm brown eyes too vivid in her mind. As she walked through the lobby, unsure what to do with herself, she spotted Quinn walking toward her. He looked so sexy in his well-cut charcoal suit, white shirt, and burgundy tie, errant strands of his light-brown hair falling across his forehead.

Quinn smiled when he saw her, his deep sea blue eyes twinkling. "Hey there. Where's J.M.?"

"I don't know," she answered. "I'm not sure what he's planning for this evening."

His eyebrow arched upward. "Really. Well, I was thinking of going out for a drink. Want to join me?"

The alternative was going to her room and being alone with her thoughts, spiraling in an endless cycle of guilt and confusion.

"That would be nice."

"I was thinking of trying a little pub a few people told me about. I'll have to go to my room and get my coat. Want to join me?"

"Sure."

She wondered if Quinn would suggest they have a little intimate diversion before they went out, or invite her to stay the night afterward. If he did, would she say yes? It would certainly keep her distracted. But she couldn't do that to J.M.

They rode the elevator up to the tenth floor. When she stepped into the hallway, she realized this was the same floor as J.M.'s. The conference organizers had arranged a block of rooms for attendees and those seemed to be concentrated on two floors. Hesitantly, she accompanied Quinn to the right, down the hall. Then they turned left, Quinn chatting all the way. She tensed as they walked down the corridor with J.M.'s room . . . held her breath as they passed J.M.'s room on the right . . . then continued four rooms down.

"Here we are." Quinn slid his key card into the slot, but the light flashed red.

Oh, please just open. Kara glanced toward J.M.'s door, praying it wouldn't open . . . or that J.M. wouldn't appear suddenly in the hall heading back to his room.

"Darn thing doesn't always work." Quinn slid the card into the slot again and drew it out more slowly. This time the light flashed green and he turned the doorknob and pushed the door open.

"There we go," he said.

Kara rushed into the room, desperate to be out of sight.

J.M. heard Quinn's voice outside, traveling along the hall. He had hoped to find Quinn and arrange to go for a drink. He could really use someone to talk to. He peered out the peephole to see who Quinn was with.

His heart stalled as he saw Kara walking along beside Quinn. Damn it, why was Kara up here with Quinn? He heard their voices stop outside Quinn's room, then disappear inside. He could hear the sound of the door latching behind them.

Kara was going to spend the night with Quinn. His

heart thundered in his chest as he realized he'd lost her. Her words echoed through his mind. *You want me to tell you I love you, but . . . I just can't do that. I can't lie to you and tell you I feel something I don't.*

No, he hadn't *lost* her. He'd never really had her.

How could he have been so wrong? Everything he'd thought about her being his soul mate—his perfect woman— had just been wishful thinking. Once again, J.M. had put his whole heart on the line. And once again, he just wasn't good enough. Would he ever learn?

He pulled his suitcase from the closet, set it on the bed, and began to pack. He couldn't bear seeing Kara and Quinn together for the rest of the week. It would just twist the knife further. He needed to get home, where he could nurse his wounds in peace.

Twenty

Kara stood by the door, annoyed by the tingle of nerves dancing through her body. Or was it desire? Did she want to be with Quinn tonight?

Quinn tossed his key on his dresser, then tugged his conference badge from his jacket and tossed it beside the key.

"If you don't mind, I'll take a minute to change."

He pulled off his suit jacket and draped it over the back of the nearest chair, then discarded his tie. When he began to unfasten his shirt buttons and she saw the smooth flesh of his broad chest slowly revealed, she tugged on her lower lip.

Did he just want to change or was he sending her a message? That he was available? Ready if she wanted him?

He tossed the white shirt on the bed, then stepped toward her. Hormones flickered through her body at the sight of his broad chest closing in on her . . . his strong, masculine arms that would be just as capable of offering comfort as they would of holding her tight while he made love to her . . . as he had so many times this week.

She wanted to melt into those arms. To lose herself in the pleasure of his lovemaking.

Or did she just want to escape her thoughts of J.M.?

"I'll be back in a minute." Quinn disappeared into the bathroom and she walked to the window and stared out into the darkness.

A few minutes later, he returned with his hair brushed neatly and smelling delicately of musky aftershave. He placed his hands on her shoulders. The gentle heat washed through her. Comforting. She cupped his cheeks and pushed herself on her toes. But at the first touch of her mouth on his, she knew this was wrong. All she could think of was J.M.

"Do you want to stay here, Kara?"

She stared into the depths of his sea blue eyes and saw acceptance. Understanding. He cared about her in a loving, friendly way. But he didn't *love* her. She could be with him and not worry about hurting him. *Or being hurt?*

He moved to kiss her again, but she dodged out of the way.

Oh, damn. She couldn't do this. She wanted J.M., not Quinn. It wouldn't be fair to treat Quinn as a surrogate. Not for him. Not for her.

"I'm sorry, Quinn. I can't do this. I'm in love with J.M." She gasped and covered her mouth, shocked at the words that had just spilled from her lips. Then she repeated them softly, more to herself than to Quinn. "I'm in love with J.M."

She stepped back from Quinn.

"I'm sorry. I hope I haven't led you on."

He rested his hand on her shoulder, the comforting heat steadying her.

"Not at all. J.M. really loves you. Do you know that? And it's clear you love him."

"Did he tell you that?" She didn't even know what she meant to ask. That he loved her? That she loved him? What did it matter?

"No, he didn't tell me. I can see it. When he looks at you. When he makes love to you. And the way you respond to him. It's clear as day that you two are meant to be together."

"Up until this week, I didn't believe in love."

He shrugged. "Well, it obviously believes in you. The loving energy pulsing through the two of you is palpable." He tucked his finger under her chin and tipped it up, then kissed her. "Don't worry about me, doll. We all had a good time. I wouldn't change a thing."

Kara knocked on J.M.'s door. There was no reply, so she knocked again . . . and again . . . and again. "J.M., are you in there? Please be in there. There's something I really need to tell you."

No response.

"J.M.?" She knocked again.

Had she hurt him so much he'd left the conference? Her heart clenched at the thought.

A sinking feeling began in the pit of her stomach. "Damn it," she muttered as she raced toward the lobby. Once there, she scanned the area. No J.M.

She hurried through the hotel bar, scanning the faces for J.M.'s. She checked the gym. The pool. Still no sign of him.

As she entered the lobby again, across the large expanse she saw J.M. walking out the front doors, his suitcase in tow. She gasped, then raced across the lobby and out the front doors—heedless of the cold and snow—just in time to see J.M. get into a taxi. She called his name as she ran toward him, but he didn't hear her over the sound of an ambulance siren blaring by and he closed the door. Luckily, the cab ahead of his stayed put while the emergency vehicle sped past, so she reached his cab before it started moving and slapped his window to get his attention, leaving her palm pressed against the glass. J.M. glanced up at her in surprise.

"J.M.," she panted. "I need to talk to you. There's something I need to tell you."

Though J.M. wouldn't be able to hear her through the glass, he seemed to understand her intent. He leaned over and said a few words to the driver, then slowly stepped out of the cab.

Kara continued to pant, trying to catch her breath. She realized she must look like a madwoman, but she had more important concerns right now.

"You told me you loved me and . . ." Her gaze dropped from his. "I was just surprised. You caught me off guard, but it doesn't mean . . . I don't feel the same way about you."

Understanding filled J.M.'s gaze. "You think I would stop loving you. Just like you believe your father did."

He drew her to his body and held her close, his strong, warm arms wrapping around her. His big hand cupped her head and held it to him, her ear nestled against his chest. She could hear his heart beating and the gentle rhythm soothed her.

She just stood here, taking comfort from his embrace, not allowing herself to think.

"I won't stop loving you, Kara." He kissed the top of her head, his lips brushing her hair tenderly. "I will never stop loving you."

Tears welled in her eyes.

"You are my perfect woman."

She shook her head, knowing she couldn't believe that.

"But I'm not perfect. I make mistakes. I have flaws. Maybe you're just seeing what you want to see."

"I didn't say you must *be* perfect. I said you're perfect *for* me." He hugged her tighter, then stroked her hair behind her ear. "Believe me, Kara. I will love you forever."

Tears streamed down her face.

"Tell me, Kara. Do you love me?"

Her throat tightened, choking back any words. He tipped her chin up and gazed at her.

"Do you love me?" he asked again.

Staring into his intense brown eyes, she could not lie. She opened her mouth, but no sound came out.

He kissed her, his solid lips caressing hers with such sweet tenderness it tore at her heart. If he ever stopped loving her . . . If he ever left her . . . How would she survive?

"I know you're afraid of being vulnerable. Afraid I'll fall out of love with you. But that will never happen. I promise you that."

She shook her head. "You can't know. . . . You can't."

"I will *never* stop loving you." He held her close. "And I will never stop doing what it takes to make our relationship work. With the two of us totally committed to doing that, we can't fail."

She drew in a breath, mesmerized by his words. She would do anything to make this relationship work. She *needed* this relationship to work. Because the alternative—living without J.M.—was simply unacceptable.

Gazing into his dark eyes, she saw the love there. Recognized what it was for the first time. A mirror of her own powerful feelings for him.

She brushed her hand across his cheek. The delicate contact sent shivers through her.

"Oh, J.M., I love you, too."

The smile that spread across his face had enough wattage to light an entire city. His lips captured hers in an exciting burst of passion. Her heart leapt in joy and she flung her arms around him and held on tight.

Twenty-one

Back in her hotel room, as his mouth moved on hers, his strong arms holding her tight, and his solid chest crushing her breasts, Kara's joy turned to yearning. She grabbed the hem of her top and pulled it up, releasing J.M.'s lips to drag it over her head. Then she tossed it away and slid her hand around the back of his neck and dragged him into another kiss. With her other hand, she flicked open the buttons of his shirt, then glided her hand along the hard ridges of his stomach. She glided her fingers to his belt, then dipped under the fabric.

She loved this man! Happiness swelled within her.

J.M. unfastened his belt, then his pants. She glided her hand over the cotton of his black briefs. His cock was hard and ready. He wanted her as much as she wanted him. She hooked her fingers under the elastic and pushed down his briefs and pants at the same time, crouching in front of him. She smiled at his large swollen erection in front of her. She wrapped her fingers around it, loving the solid feel of his thick shaft in her hand. She touched the tip of her tongue to his cockhead, teasing it. Flicking her tongue over the end, then spiraling around until she circled the ridge beneath the corona.

He groaned. She wrapped her lips around him and swallowed the mushroom tip into her mouth, then squeezed. She sucked as she glided her hand up and down, then tucked her other hand under his cock and stroked his balls.

J.M. grasped her shoulders and eased her upward, his eyes blazing with emotion, then stormed her mouth with his until she gasped for breath. He reached behind her and unfastened her bra, then drew it from her body. He dipped down and sucked her nipple until it throbbed with need.

Her hand found his cock again and she stroked while he sucked. Soon he scooped her up and carried her to the bed. When he set her down, they both shed the rest of their clothes, then she sat on the bed and he knelt in front of her. Her insides contracted with need as he slid his hands under her knees and tucked them over his shoulders, then kissed along her thighs, heading toward her wet opening.

The moment his mouth touched her there, she gasped. His tongue pressed into her as he brushed his thumb over her clit. Her fingers tangled in his hair and her breathing accelerated.

"Oh, God." Intense sensations shot through her. He licked, then his tongue dove into her again and again as his thumb flicked over her sensitive bud.

Bliss

She moaned as waves of ecstatic pleasure washed through her, blossoming into an incredible orgasm.

She pulled him toward her, then cradled his face between her hands and kissed him. His cock nudged her slick opening, then she gasped as he glided into her while she still sat on the edge of the bed.

"Wrap your legs around me, sweetheart."

She wrapped her legs around his waist, allowing his cock to sink deeper. She squeezed him inside, anticipating his first deep thrust. But instead, he tucked his hands under her butt and lifted her, then sank to the floor, where he sat cross-legged. With their arms around each other, she sitting in the cradle of his thighs, she felt extremely close to him. Open. Vulnerable. Yet safe.

He kissed her again.

Her breasts pressed tight against his chest and their hearts thumping in unison made her feel incredibly close to him, not to mention her vagina wide open and filled by his marble-hard cock.

She squeezed him inside her.

"You know, this is the perfect position to have an energy orgasm together with a physical orgasm."

Her eyes widened. "Really? You can do that?"

He smiled, the warmth in his loving gaze melting her heart. "With your legs wrapped around me, you are open wide, so my thrusts go deeper. It also aligns our chakras, so we are even more intimately linked."

She squeezed him again, tightening around his hard shaft. She had so much to learn from this man.

She began to rock. His cock glided out and in slightly with each tilt of her pelvis. She drew in deep breaths, matching his rhythm.

"As you breathe, think of the air as energy moving through both our bodies, not just yours."

She felt the energy moving through her, circling through J.M., then through her again, until it became a continuous circle. She felt incredibly close to him, as if they were one body.

"Now think of energy moving up your body from your base into your sacral."

As he talked her through moving the energy up her body, his hand followed, his loving touch igniting a fire in each of her chakras until she gasped for air. Heat rippled through her, setting her cells ablaze. Her nipples swelled, pressing into his hard chest. Her intimate muscles gripped his thick cock tightly as fire scorched through her sex . . . up through her body . . . and sparked out the crown of her head.

Intensely aware of J.M.'s body pressed tight to hers, her legs embracing him, she felt totally at one with him. She gasped at the intensity of the flood of pleasure racing through her, then expanding outward, filling every part of her . . . of them . . . with pure bliss. Time seemed to freeze as every cell in her body exploded with intense joy. A joy she shared with the man she loved.

Her entire body trembled. And her soul resonated with an infinite sense of being at one with all things. Ecstasy filled her. Filled J.M. And the universe around them.

Just as she felt the bliss was subsiding, another wave pummeled through her and she gasped again. A flood of liquid heat erupted from J.M. into her, expanding her pleasure yet again. She arched against him, flying beyond consciousness, flying through a black void of pure, unadulterated ecstasy.

She awoke to J.M. kissing her, unsure where she was exactly.

Sitting?

She realized J.M.'s cock still impaled her as she sat in his lap.

"What happened?" she asked.

He grinned broadly. "You're a natural at this. You just reached an enlightened state that allowed you to transcend the physical realm."

She blinked. "I beg your pardon?"

His eyes twinkled. "You blacked out."

She rested her head against his solid shoulder. "Well, it felt pretty good."

He rocked his pelvis forward. "Just pretty good?"

Heat thrummed through her again at the feel of his rock-hard cock gliding along her vagina.

"Pretty *damn* good."

He chuckled, then pressed her back until she lay on the carpet. He drove his cock deep and she moaned, clinging to his shoulders. He thrust again and again. Deeper. Harder.

She gasped and moaned as she sailed off to the realm of ecstatic pleasure yet again. J.M. groaned and filled her yet again.

She clutched J.M. tight to her body as she lay breathless. "This Tantra stuff is not bad at all."

She gazed up at him, then cupped his cheeks in her hands. "And the Tantra master is pretty damn special, too," she said, and kissed him with passion and unadulterated love.

When she finally released his lips, the loving warmth in his eyes filled her with pure bliss. He tightened his arm around her waist and she snuggled against him, knowing in her heart that what she shared with J.M. was a love that would last forever.

Read on for a preview of Opal Carew's
upcoming erotic romance

Pleasure Bound

Available from St. Martin's Griffin in Fall 2010

Ty was once a master of domination, but a bad experience led him to change his lifestyle. When he falls in love with Marie, he plans to handle her with kid gloves. Unfortunately, Marie thinks Ty is too nice of a guy to be the overpowering Dominant she dreams of. When Ty's old friend Zeke enters the scene, he's more than happy to give Marie exactly what she wants. But when Zeke starts to experience feelings for Ty that he's never allowed to surface before, it could push all three of them to the edge . . .

Images of the sexy bad boy from the next cottage haunted Marie as she stepped from the cottage onto the wooden deck and glanced across the tranquil lake. She took a deep breath of fresh country air as she walked down the deck stairs and headed toward the water. She wanted to sit on the beach and enjoy the sunrise in quiet solitude before other cottagers were up and about. Maybe take a refreshing dip in the calm water.

Of course, if she happened to run into the gorgeous guy from next door, that would be quite fine.

She liked his name. Zeke. It was different from the names of the men she dated. Of course, Zeke was a *completely* different type of man. The men she'd dated were very nice. Dependable. Confident. Pleasant. Although she'd only spoken with Zeke briefly, and it had been friendly and pleasant, she could sense in him an aura of . . . danger. No, that wasn't quite right. She felt safe around him. Protected almost. It was more as if he would like to . . . dominate her. That he would take control and totally master her. Which sent tingles through her.

It's not anything he'd said. In fact, it was probably more a matter of how she reacted to his extremely masculine presence. And a result of their first encounter. Marie's friend Sylvia had invited her to the cottage for the Labor Day weekend. They'd arrived last night and had been enjoying a quiet evening under the stars roasting marshmallows and talking. As much as they could with a wild party going on at the next cottage with a tough-looking crowd. Marie had never seen so many tattoos and body-piercings in one group of people. As the evening progressed, the music had gotten louder and the partygoers more drunk. When tempers flared and a fight broke out, Zeke had shown up out of nowhere.

At first, Marie and Sylvia had thought Zeke was one of

them, in his tight jeans and black T-shirt, with a tattoo along his arm and the two spike piercings in his eyebrow, but he'd turned out to be more like a knight in shining armor. He'd settled them down, promising to bust their butts if they acted up again. He had an air of authority that they couldn't ignore.

Nor could she. A knight in shining armor was nice, and she was glad he'd been on hand, but the bad boy aura was a total turn on! He'd stopped by their cottage afterward to see if they were okay, explaining he was in the cottage two doors down. He'd come to the lake to enjoy some solitude. They'd invited him in for a drink and chatted for a half hour, then he'd headed out.

She sighed as she walked past a clump of bushes toward the secluded patch of beach Sylvia had shown her yesterday. Birds chirped in the trees, the water swished against the shore, and the haunting cry of a loon sounded in the distance.

Her beach towel draped over her shoulder, she slipped between the bushes to the quiet inlet . . . then stopped cold. A man was wading into the water. He had a large tattoo of a fierce-looking dragon arched along his back, another tattoo coiling along his arm and over his shoulder, and a black tribal band around the other bicep.

And . . . he was completely butt naked!

And a fine butt it was. She couldn't help watching the muscles ripple as he stepped forward. As if sensing her presence, he stopped then turned around. She felt her cheeks burning at having been caught ogling him, but he simply smiled, revealing beautiful white teeth. That square jaw and those rich olive green eyes . . . it was Zeke. How could she not have recognized the golden serpentine body of a dragon tattooed along his upper arm and disappearing over his shoulder? Of course, she had been busy admiring those hard, tight buttocks.

The whole time they'd chatted at the cottage last night, Marie had wondered what the rest of that tattoo, which had disappeared under the sleeve of his T-shirt, looked like. In fact, she'd wondered what it would be like to see him naked, as well as what it would feel like to have his lips pressed hard to hers. Now, she knew. At least, the naked part.

As he watched her, his cock hardened and rose. Man, his butt was fine, but his cock was absolutely sensational! Enormous. She'd love to . . .

"Join me." His words, almost matter-of-fact, held a spine-tingling tone of authority.

Mesmerized, she dropped her towel and walked toward him. Tremors rippled across her flesh as she got closer. He held out his hand and she took it, then he tugged her toward him and drew her into his arms. She sucked in a breath as her bikini-clad body came in contact with his hard masculine body. Naked flesh to naked flesh. He smiled a devilish grin, then captured her lips.

His mouth, firm and confident, moved on hers with quiet authority. When his tongue brushed her lips she opened and he invaded her firmly and thoroughly.

Breathless, she stepped back and stared at him in awe. He scooped her up and carried her into the water, his lips merging with hers again.

It was sweet heaven. He was so . . . masculine. So . . . powerful. Yet she felt totally safe with him.

The water caressed first her bottom, then more of her . . . cool . . . but she barely noticed. As he continued deeper, the water surrounding them, he released her legs and she curled around until she faced him, then she wrapped her legs around him. His hard cock nestled between them, pressing against her. Oh God, she wanted this man. She didn't care that they'd just met. That she never had sex with a man until at least five dates. She wanted him. Here and now. What was wrong with being a little wild and crazy every now and again? Why couldn't she do something totally out of character?

She reached down to her bikini bottom and untied the strings holding it together at the sides, then tugged the scrap of fabric away. He grinned at the obvious invitation . . .

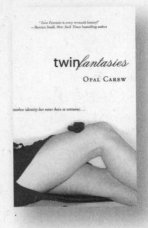

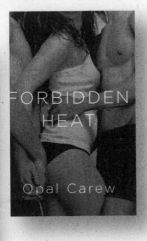